WILD STORIES

WILD STORIES

Text and illustrations by

Colin Thompson

RANDOM HOUSE AUSTRALIA

Visit Colin Thompson's website: http://www.colinthompson.com

This work is fictitious. Any resemblance to anyone living or dead is purely coincidental.

A Random House book
Published by Random House Australia Pty Ltd
Level 3, 100 Pacific Highway, North Sydney NSW 2060
www.randomhouse.com.au

This collection first published in the United States by Kane Miller in 2010
First published in Australia by Random House Australia in 2010

Addresses for companies within the Random House Group can be found at
www.randomhouse.com.au/offices.

A Cataloguing-in-Publication Entry is available from the National Library of
Australia

ISBN: 978 1 86471 826 3

Design, illustrations and typesetting by Colin Thompson
Additional typesetting by Anna Warren, Warren Ventures Pty Ltd

10 9 8 7 6 5 4 3

Printed and bound by The SOS Print + Media Group

FSC
Mixed Sources
Product group from well-managed
forests and other controlled sources
Cert no. SGS-COC-3047
www.fsc.org
© 1996 Forest Stewardship Council

The paper this book is printed on is certified by
the ©1996 Forest Stewardship Council A.C.
(FSC). SOS Print + Media Group holds FSC
chain of custody certification
(Cert no. SGS-COC-3047).

FSC promotes environmentally responsible,
socially beneficial and economically viable
management of the world's forests.

For my grandsons Walter and Donald

and

to the memory of Margery Fisher (1913–1992) who,
in the first review I ever got, said that *Ethel the Chicken*
was a masterpiece. It was the most wonderful start to my
writing career.

Table of Contents

BOOK 3

INTRODUCTION

The first story I ever wrote was called *Ethel the Chicken*.

It was published in 1991 and in 1993 it was published again with some more stories in a book called *Sid the Mosquito & Other Wild Stories*.

In 1995 I had a second book of stories published called *Attila the Bluebottle & More Wild Stories*, and in 1996 there was a third book called *Venus the Caterpillar & Further Wild Stories*.

These three books were only published in the UK and all three went out of print several years ago.

Although Ethel the chicken sort of died in the third book, she went on to have an exciting career in five more books. She re-appeared as a ghost in *The Haunted Suitcase*. She turned up as a not very good reincarnation in *Castle Twilight* and as an extremely wise old bird in *The Puzzle Duck*. Then her career really took off when she appeared as an all-powerful super-intelligent being from outer space trapped inside a chicken's body in *Future Eden* and again in the sequel *Space – The Final Effrontery.*

Unfortunately none of these books are available any more, but to prove that Ethel the chicken is immortal, I'm delighted to say that Ethel and all the stories from Sid, Attila and Venus are here again in one big book.

BOOK 1

Sleep

At the end of a quiet street, at the edge of a large town, stood a beautiful old house. The honeysuckle grew high around its walls and the paint curled up at the edges of the windows. Behind the dusty glass, dark velvet curtains brushed against a forest of cobwebs and at the back of the house a wide lawn led down to a tangle of fruit trees and a forgotten pond.

At the top of the street the traffic hurried by but in this short road that led to nowhere it was peaceful and quiet.

Around the house and lawn, tall trees and thick bushes grew wonderful and wild with birds and creatures and insects that flashed in the flickering sunlight. Hedgehogs slipped beneath overgrown branches, watched from the cellar windows by dark brown rats. Mosquitos hovered over the lawn in the misty haze of summer and from beneath the eaves of the house swallows swooped down to catch them. At the bottom of the garden there were rabbits and in the tops of the trees there were squirrels.

An old lady and an old dog lived in the house.

They had lived there all their lives. The old lady had been born there when the house had been bright and new and full of people. With her brothers and sisters she had run through the rooms, and every corner of the house had been full of sunshine and laughter.

Everyone else was gone now. Her mother and father had died a long time ago and her brothers and sisters all lived far away in other towns.

The old lady and the dog and the house had grown old together. Twelve years ago, her nephew, who thought she might be lonely, had bought her the dog. For the first time in her long life the old lady had someone who needed her. And for the first time in years the house was filled with words as she talked to her new friend.

'Shall we go and pick some flowers?' she would say, or, 'Time for a cup of tea, I think.'

Every morning the old lady opened the back door and the old dog shuffled out into the garden. He sniffed the dustbin, lifted his face to the sky to catch the smells of the day and then set off round his territory.

'Morning,' said the weasels as he passed their hole in the wall.

'Morning,' said the dog as he ambled by.

'Nice day,' said the mole.

'It's raining,' said the dog.

'Yes, but it's nice rain.'

The dog was always surprised to see the mole. No matter what time of day he went round the garden, she would be there, just coming out of her hole. What he didn't know was that she was lonely and listened for his footsteps across the lawn. She thought he was wonderful and as he walked across the grass she scampered beneath him down her tunnels so that she could pop up as he went by.

'Morning,' said the dog to the old chicken who lived in a box at the bottom of the lawn. The chicken was even older than he was and when he went by she was usually fast asleep and didn't answer.

As he passed the dark wooden shed where the lawnmower and the deckchairs were kept, he pushed his nose into the hole where the hedgehogs lived.

'It's raining,' he said into the dark space under the shed. His daily weather report was usually met with sleepy grunts. Most of the hedgehogs slept all day, particularly if it was raining. Some of the young ones were often about, snuffling in the dandelions for slugs, but it was very rare to see an adult hedgehog before mid-afternoon.

The dog moved on to the bottom of the garden where there was a rusty car that had once taken the old lady to school. Now it was full of ferns and mice who lived behind the dashboard.

'I do wish he wouldn't do that,' they said when the dog lifted his leg against the front tyre.

'I know,' said a sparrow who had built her nest in the glove compartment. 'It lowers the tone of the whole neighbourhood.'

As the dog walked under the tall sycamore trees, the crows that nested high up in the top branches called down to him.

'Good morning, dog,' they cried.

'What? Who said that?' said the dog, looking round. It was the same every day. He never thought of looking up towards the sky and he had begun to believe the trees were haunted. The crows thought the dog was stupid and shouted to him each day as a joke.

Past the car was the rabbit warren. The dog didn't know what to make of the rabbits. He was a gentle, quiet animal and the rabbits were loud and rough, not at all like rabbits are supposed to be. Large eyes peered out of the holes as he went by. Rabbits are supposed to be frightened of dogs but these laughed and whistled and he kept away from them.

He ambled through the orchard, sometimes eating a fallen apple, before coming out onto the lawn again and wandering up to the back door where he sat and barked until the old lady let him in.

On summer days the old lady opened the French windows at the back of the house and the dog went out to lie in the sunshine. He lay in the middle of the lawn and got hotter and hotter until he was panting like a steam train. Then he would go to the pond for a drink and come back to lie under the bushes.

'You know,' he said to a hedgehog as they lay together under a gooseberry bush, 'my human's amazing. I'd swear she understands my every thought.' Across the lawn, the old lady was sitting by the open door knitting a blue blanket.

'Yes,' agreed the hedgehog. 'She's almost doglike.'

'You're absolutely right,' said the dog. 'I mean,

look at her now. How does she know my favourite colour's blue? Yet there she is, knitting me a blue blanket.'

'She's a great credit to you,' said the hedgehog. 'You must feel very proud.'

'Well, one does one's best.'

When people and animals get old, they need to be cared for. Houses are the same. But as gardens grow old, they become more beautiful each year. The less people interfere with them, the better they become. If a tree falls and someone clears it away, it's gone forever. If it's left alone, it becomes home to a thousand insects and creeping plants. Fungus grows and the tree slowly melts back into the earth to feed new trees.

When the old lady and the house had been young, the garden was already full of ancient trees. Her father had planted more and now they were full grown.

Beneath the trees and bushes, weeds grew thick in tiny jungles. Nettles and dandelions brought butterflies and birds to the garden and behind the secret leaves mice and frogs lived hidden lives.

When the old lady's nephew came he cut the

lawn, but apart from that the garden was left to grow its own way. All around, the other houses had neat tidy rows of flowers, sprayed and weeded in lifeless earth, but here was a complete world where nature lived unharmed.

The lily pond was hidden behind overgrown raspberry canes. The vegetable garden had disappeared under a carpet of grass. When she had been a little girl, the old lady had planted radishes there, in between her father's lettuces. Now even the brick paths had vanished under a coat of moss. Nature wrapped the whole garden in a beautiful blanket and then started on the house.

'That's nice,' said the old lady, when she saw little trees growing in the gutters and ivy creeping across the window sills.

The dog was very old now and as the summer passed he grew slower and slower. He slept more and more and his dreams of the days when he could jump and play grew faint and quiet. His rubber ball lay behind the armchair collecting dust. The air around him grew still and weary. Nature sighed and waited. The wind slammed the door unheard and the sweet smells of the garden flowed over him unnoticed. In the garden, the animals passed the open doors and saw him lying there far away in his peaceful silence. The mole waited quietly in her tunnel but he no longer took his daily walk. As the first gold leaves of autumn began to fall he climbed into his bed and went to sleep forever.

He was buried beneath the red apple tree that the old lady had planted as a child, and when her nephew had smoothed over the sad little mound and put the spade back among the dark cobwebs and broken deck-chairs in the garden shed, they went back to the house and packed her bags.

'It's time for a change,' she said and went to live by the sea. The house stayed behind and went to sleep.

The lawn grew tall and thick and criss-crossed with the tunnels of animals that had grown up in the shadows and now came out into the open. The creatures that had hidden in the cellars moved up into the empty rooms and as the years passed, the wild garden grew wilder until the house called fourteen lay hidden behind a wall of green.

The Old Dog

He sits by the door
And looks out at the rain
As it falls soft and warm on the lawn.
The summer has nearly faded again
And each winter comes with a little more pain
And a little less fight for the storm.

He sits by the door
Looking right through the rain
At a spot on the far side of space.
He's getting tired of taking the strain,
There are lights going out in the back of his brain,
He's content to withdraw from the race.

Sid the Mosquito

Behind the trees at the end of the lawn, the pond lay hidden by overgrown bushes. The trees hung their branches down to touch the water and at the water's edge tall grass grew full of hidden flowers and butterflies. Birds flashed across the water catching flies and their voices filled the air with music.

Dragonflies danced in the air like sparkling jewels unseen by anyone except the mice and birds who went to drink at the water's edge. In the pond itself little creatures lived their secret lives. Tiny snails wriggled in the soft mud at the bottom of the pond.

Water beetles and worms darted between the roots of waterlilies. Beneath the top of the water, mosquito larvae hung like baby caterpillars waiting to become butterflies. Then very early one morning, before the sun was even up, they all changed into mosquitos and flew off into the jungle of soft grass that grew beneath the honeysuckle.

'Can I go and bite something now, Mum?' said a young mosquito called Sid.

'No, dear,' said his mother.

'Oh go on, Mum,' said Sid. 'Everyone knows mosquitos bite things.'

'Not boys,' said his mother. 'Boys don't bite things, only girls do that.' All Sid's sisters giggled and nudged each other and pointed.

'But what am I going to have for my breakfast if I can't bite something?' cried Sid.

'You have to suck pollen out of buttercups, you do,' sneered his eldest sister, and they all giggled again.

'It's not true,' said Sid with tears in his eyes, but it was. His mother tried to explain as gently as she could that boy mosquitos and girl mosquitos were made differently and that with his delicate mouth he just wouldn't be able to bite anything.

'You just go and get your head into a nice dandelion,' she said.

'I'm not sucking soppy flowers,' said Sid. 'Everyone'll laugh at me.'

'No they won't,' said his mother. 'Your father loved pollen. Why, he spent half his life with his head buried in bluebells.'

Sid felt as if someone had played a rotten trick on him. It had been no fun wiggling around in the pond as a larva, dodging out of the way of the horrid dragonflies and the drinking dog and swimming around with his ears full of stagnant water and hedgehog spit. It had been no fun at all and the only thing that had kept him going had been the thought of biting a nice soft human leg. And now they were telling him that all he was going to get was soppy flowers.

'And keep away from the roses until you're grown up,' she added. 'They're much too strong for a young lad like you.'

The sun climbed above the house, sending its clear light through the branches above the pond. The air grew warmer and one by one Sid's sisters all flew off to bite things. While his mother went down to the shops to bite a greengrocer, Sid kicked his feet in the earth and sulked under a nettle all morning. There was no way he was going to put his head inside a flower and that was final. He was going to bite a human, or at least the dog. He would even settle for a small mouse but certainly not a dandelion.

The morning became the afternoon and Sid grew hungrier and hungrier. As his sisters came and went with tales of blood they had drunk from policemen's necks and sparrows' knees, Sid listened to his tummy rumble until at last he could stand it no longer.

As soon as no one was looking, he flew off to the house next door to bite a baby.

Noises and new smells floated out of the open windows. There were humans inside, laughing and talking and eating. Sid landed on the window sill and looked at their bare arms. There was a big pink juicy baby sitting on the floor sucking a sock. Sid was about to fly down to it when he noticed one of his three hundred and five sisters sitting on someone's ear. As he watched, a hand flashed through the air and squashed her. Sid turned and fled.

In the garden the dog snored gently under a deckchair and Sid decided it would be safer to start with him. He landed on the grass, tiptoed across to the sleeping animal, shut his eyes and pounced.

The next thing he knew, he was flying through the air with a sore nose and tears streaming from his eyes.

'Get out of it,' growled an angry voice in the dog's fur.

'Yeah,' said another, 'or we'll pull your wings off.'

'Yeah, that's right,' said a third.

Sid sat up and shook his head. Something dark and horrible leapt out of the dog and landed in front of him. It was an angry flea with a mean look in its eye.

'Listen sonny,' it said, 'that's our dog that is, so watch it. You just push off back to the buttercups where you belong.'

'Yeah, push off,' the third flea said again from somewhere behind the dog's left ear.

Sid crept off into the quiet heart of a big red rose bush and hid behind a sharp thorn. He could hear the fleas all laughing but after a while the dog got up and wandered off and it was peaceful again. His nose was still very sore and he really was very hungry by then so, forgetting his mother's advice, he stuck his tongue into the middle of a big red rose.

His mouth was filled with a million wonderful

tastes. The pollen tasted like strawberry jam, caramel pudding and black cherry ice cream all rolled into one. As he wriggled his tongue around he picked up the nectar which was even more wonderful, like thick chocolate sauce and crème eggs floating in condensed milk. Of course, Sid was only a little mosquito and had never heard of chocolate or all the other delicious things. All he knew was that what he was eating was totally amazingly completely fantastic and he was feeling sick.

In no time at all, he was so full up he couldn't fly. He staggered around in the grass with a silly grin on his face and finally bumped into his mother.

'Hello, Mummy,' he mumbled and fell flat on his back. He lay there waving his legs in the air and singing a little song.

'Sidney, you've been in the rose bush, haven't you?' said his mother, pretending to be cross.

'Hello, Mummy,' he said again.

'And what's happened to your nose? Have you been fighting?'

'Big flea bashed me,' said Sid and fell fast asleep. Soon he was far away in the land of dreams where huge roses grew as big as flying saucers. The air was filled with raindrops only they weren't raindrops, they were drops of nectar.

Sid dreamt he was floating down a river of nectar in a little boat made of a rose petal. He passed a raft of grass that was sinking fast and the three nasty fleas on board couldn't swim. They cried out for him to save them but he just poked his tongue out at them and sailed by.

On the riverbanks, children with big soft pink arms begged him to come and bite them as he passed, but he couldn't stop because he was on his way to a special appointment. He dreamt that the Queen of England herself had sent him a telegram requesting his presence at Buckingham Palace where he was to bite Her Majesty's left ear, and for pudding he was to have a go at all the royal corgis.

When Sid woke up, it really was raining. His mother had bitten off a piece of grass and covered him with it so only his feet sticking out of the bottom were getting wet. Like all insects everywhere he climbed up under a leaf to keep dry and sat next to an old spider, waiting for the rain to pass. The spider kept complaining that when she was a girl it was always nice and sunny and never rained at all.

By the time the sky was clear again, evening was falling and Sid's sisters began to come home. Some flew in alone, some came in twos or threes and other arrived in groups.

Twenty-seven of the sisters hadn't come back yet as they were biting people at a barbecue in next door's garden. Fourteen had been squashed, twelve had discovered too late what it is that swallows swallow and one had got stuck to some sticky tape on a parcel and was on her way to Australia.

Young lady mosquitos are horrible things. They bite anything they can get their nasty teeth into. They bite sleeping babies, happy budgerigars and even princesses. And when there's nothing else to bite they bite each other. Sid sat quietly in the corner and listened as the girls sat around telling amazing stories.

'I bit the postman three times,' said one.

'That's nothing,' said one called Sharon. 'I flew right into a bathroom and bit an enormous lady with no clothes on seven times and I tripped over the soap and bruised three of my knees really badly.'

'Well, that's nothing at all,' boasted a third sister. 'I flew into an aeroplane, went all the way to America and back and bit twenty-three first-class passengers.'

'You're all dead soft, you are,' said the stupidest sister. 'I'm so tough I jumped up and down inside the prickliest thistle in the whole world and bit myself twenty-seven million million times.'

They went on for hours boasting away to each other, each sister trying to be braver and cleverer than the others. Sid listened wide-eyed to their stories. He was an honest little insect and didn't realise they were making them all up. Even when one said she had been to the moon in a spaceship, he believed her.

'And what have you been doing?' they asked Sid. As well as biting everything, young lady mosquitos are very rude to everyone, have dreadful bad breath and lots of spots. Young boy mosquitos on the other hand, because they only eat nectar and pollen, are kind and well behaved and have perfect skin.

'Have you been fighting a ferocious buttercup?' laughed the girls.

'You leave young Sid alone,' said his mother. 'He's had more adventures today than any of you.'

'Ooh, ooh,' sneered the sisters. 'Did you get slapped by a daisy?'

'He got hit on the nose by some vicious fleas and doesn't want any trouble from you lot.'

'Fleas, fleas. We hate fleas,' shouted the girls and they all flew off to fight them, except Sharon who stayed behind to rub a dock leaf on her sore knees.

The next morning was perfect. A little cloud of soft mist hung above the pond as the sunshine crept over the trees. Birds stretched their wings and filled the air with a hundred new songs. The dragonflies flashed across the water while butterflies unfolded themselves and flew off across the nettles where busy ladybirds scuttled about. All down the little street the houses were quiet except for the clinking sound of milk bottles.

Sid sat on a twig breathing the damp sweet air. One by one his nasty sisters staggered out from under their leaves. They wandered about swearing a lot. They swore at the birds for being too noisy. They swore at the sunshine for being too bright. They swore at the butterflies for being too beautiful and they swore at the humans for still being in bed when they wanted to bite them. Most of all though, they swore at each other for being mosquitos.

Eventually they all flew off and the pond was peaceful again. Sid flew deep inside an enormous waterlily. It was like being in a great big white tent.

19

He shared his breakfast with a couple of wasps and a family of small brown beetles. One of the wasps was called Arnold and was about the same age as Sid.

Sid tried to tell Arnold about not being able to bite people but the wasp's ears were completely filled up with pollen and he couldn't hear him. Sid tried shouting.

'There's no need to shout,' said Arnold.

'Sorry.'

'What did you say?' said Arnold.

'Nothing,' muttered Sid and flew back to his twig. Nobody seemed to be interested in a little mosquito's problems. It wasn't that he didn't like pollen: it was very nice. And it wasn't that he wanted to be off with his sisters biting people all day long. All he wanted was one little bite, just to prove he could do it. That was all.

He decided to try again and set off towards the house next door. The curtains and windows were all open now. The people were cooking their breakfast and the cat was chasing birds round the edge of the lawn. As Sid sat on the kitchen window sill, Arnold shot past and dived head first into a jar of marmalade.

Sid flew upstairs and into a bedroom. Inside, a

small boy was getting dressed. Sid landed on his neck and tried to bite him. He opened his mouth as wide as he could and pushed and shoved and clenched his fists. His ears began to ache and he went bright red in the face but all he could do was dribble.

The little boy went down to the kitchen and Sid sat on the bedside table and cried.

At first there were so many tears in his eyes that he didn't notice the little man standing next to him. Then as his tears grew less he saw him. He had his back to Sid and didn't seem to have any clothes on. Sid tiptoed over and tried to bite him on the shoulder. To his amazement, his tiny teeth went right into the man and his mouth was filled with sugar.

Sid jumped for joy. Then he noticed the others. There was a whole crowd of them hiding in a box. They didn't seem to notice him at all so he went and bit every one of them. It was like sticking his head in the rose. He felt all happy and giddy. He had done it! He had actually bitten someone.

A bit later on the little boy came back and got the box of jelly babies, but by then Sid was back at the pond telling everyone about his adventure.

Three Sparrows

It was a beautiful hot summer's day and in the cluttered branches of an old apple tree three sparrows were sitting on a twig looking at a baby bird. It was a big fat creature with spiky little wings poking out of its fuzzy baby feathers. It sat hunched up in a tiny nest with a mean look in its eye.

'He's a big boy, your Andrew,' said Gladys, the first sparrow.

'Absolutely enormous,' said Mavis, his proud mother.

'In fact, he's twice as big as you.'

'Lovely, isn't he?' beamed Mavis. 'Who's Mummy's lovely boy, then?'

'He's very big for his size,' said Doris, the third sparrow.

'Shut up, Doris,' said Gladys.

'He must eat a lot,' she said.

'Eat? Eat? I'll say he eats. Never stops,' said Mavis. 'I don't get a minute's rest.'

'And the other children?' asked Gladys. 'Get on all right with him, do they?'

'Other children?'

'Well, you had five, didn't you?'

'You know, I'd forgotten all about the others,' said Mavis. 'I wonder where they've got to?'

'Probably squashed flat under your precious baby,' muttered Doris.

'What?'

'I said, he's very fat,' said Doris.

'No he's not,' snapped Mavis. 'He's big-boned.'

The young bird opened his beak and let out such a great squawk that the three sparrows fell off the branch. Instinctively Mavis dived into the bushes and came out a few seconds later with a big fat worm.

'I do wish he wouldn't grab his food like that,' said Mavis, pulling her head out of Andrew's gigantic mouth.

'He'll swallow you if you're not careful,' said Gladys.

'He seems a bit simple to me,' said Doris.

'Well, you should know,' snapped Gladys.

'He's a lovely boy,' said Mavis, hopping along the twig. 'Who's Mummy's little beauty, then?'

'Cuckoo,' said Andrew.

Ted the Flea

There are some people who think they are better than others because they talk differently or live in an expensive house. Because they've got a bigger car or more money, they look down on everyone else. It's just the same with fleas. Fleas who live on smart dogs think they are superior to fleas that live on cats. Fleas that live on rabbits think they are better than fleas that live on hedgehogs. And fleas that live on humans think they are the greatest fleas in the world.

Ted was the humblest flea of all, for he lived on a rat. It wasn't even a young bright-eyed rat but a wheezing old creature with two yellow teeth and only one ear that lived alone in a rusty tin down a drain.

'You don't know when you're well off,' said Ted's mother. 'There are fleas in China who would give their eye teeth to live in such luxury.'

'No, there aren't,' said Ted.

'I'll no-there-aren't you in a minute, my boy,' snapped his mother.

'Ungrateful, that's what he is,' cursed his granny. 'When I was his age, I er, I er,' stuttered the old flea, unable to remember.

'What?' said Ted. 'When you were my age, what?'

'Er, well, when I was your age,' spluttered his granny, 'I was younger.'

'Shut up and drink your blood,' said Ted's mother.

'It's horrible,' said Ted. 'It tastes of dirty washing-up water and mouldy bacon.'

'Ungrateful, that's what he is,' muttered his granny again. 'Children these days don't know when they're well off. When I was his age we had to live on slug dribble and glad we were to get it.'

'Yes, and ant sick,' said Ted's mother.

'Ah, the good old days,' said Ted's granny with a faraway look in her eyes.

'But I'm a vegetarian,' protested Ted.

'Don't be stupid,' snapped his mother.

That night Ted crept off to bed in the rat's scabby ear feeling very sorry for himself. He fell asleep shivering under three greasy hairs in a quilt of green wax and dreamt of a better life. Up above in the outside world it was raining. Thundering water poured down the drain, splashing into the tin as it passed, and the old rat twitched and coughed in its sleep. All night long it rained, but asleep in the rat's only ear Ted dreamt of summer fields and the sunshine that he'd never seen. While the rest of his disgusting family snored between the rat's toes, he was far away in a magical land.

The sun was shining brightly in a clear blue sky. It shone down on a field of bright red poppies and gentle grass. In the field, fluffy lambs jumped and played and deep in the wool of the prettiest lamb of all, Ted lay back as a beautiful lady flea fed him on strawberry juice.

'I was offered the chance to live in a queen's armpit,' whispered the beautiful flea in a soft French accent. 'But I turned it down so I could stay with you.'

'Oh,' sighed Ted.

'Oh,' sighed the pretty French flea.

'Oh, you bone idle little scruffbag,' shouted a voice, knocking him out of bed.

Ted's ears were still ringing an hour later from the whack his mother had given him. He sat sniffling on the rat's last remaining whisker and looked out at the wet drain. The rest of his family were having breakfast in the rat's navel but Ted just didn't feel hungry.

There must be more to life than this, he thought to himself.

Suddenly, there was a scratching noise from further down the drain and a soaking mouse came scrabbling up the brickwork. Ted saw his chance and as the mouse drew level with the tin, he sprang on to its back and held on tight as the animal climbed out into the garden and the bright spring sunshine.

'Hello,' he called quietly as he explored the mouse's fur. 'Anyone at home?' But there wasn't. He searched from the end of the mouse's tail to the tip of its nose, but there were no other fleas on board. He had the whole creature to himself.

All morning Ted sat on the mouse's head as it

bustled around the flower beds eating seeds. There was so much to take in, so many amazing things that he'd never seen before: the grass, the trees and the wonderful sunshine.

For the first time in his life he felt warm and happy. Birds, whose voices he had only heard as distant echoes at the top of the drain, flew in and out of the bushes singing to each other. There were butterflies, red roses, and golden dandelions, and across the lawn a big black cat that came nearer and nearer, tiptoeing towards them without a sound. It shone like polish and its sharp white teeth grew brighter and brighter and larger and larger until they suddenly disappeared into the mouse's fur with a snap that threw Ted high into the air.

Over and over he rolled, until he came crashing down into a world of total darkness in the cat's fur.

'Do you mind?' said a superior voice.

'Really, some people,' said another.

Gradually Ted's eyes grew used to the dark and in front of him he could see the owners of the voices. They were fleas, but quite unlike the fleas he had grown up with. They were fat and shiny, not dull and skinny like Ted's family.

'Hello,' he said, 'I'm Ted.'

'Well, Ted,' said the largest flea, looking down her nose at him. 'You can't stay here.'

'Why not?' asked Ted.

'There isn't any room.'

'But there's lots of room,' said Ted.

'No there isn't,' said the fattest flea. 'You'll have to get off.'

The more Ted protested, the nastier the fleas became. He tried crying but it did no good. They just poked him and tried to make him fall off. In the end he got angry and started calling them all the rude names he'd heard his mother use. They chased him but they were so fat they couldn't catch him. He ran off down the end of the cat's tail where they were far too stuck up to go.

After the cat had eaten the mouse it curled up under a bush and went to sleep. The air was warm and filled with the hum of summer flies. A blackbird hopped about on the lawn digging in the grass. Closer and closer it came until it was right behind the cat. As it bent over to pull a fat worm out of the earth, Ted leapt on to its back and two minutes later he was high in the sky, far above the old house and garden.

As he looked down he saw the cat come out from beneath the bush and jump over the fence into next door's garden. There were two children playing on the striped lawn and the flower beds and bushes were all trimmed and cut tidily. There were gardens like that as far as Ted could see. There were people pushing lawnmowers and hanging out washing or just sitting in the sun. In some gardens dogs lay stretched out and a few sparrows and starlings flitted about, but only the garden he had grown up in was wild and full of wonderful overgrown trees. Everywhere else was clean and tidy like a room inside a house. Only his garden was alive with birds and wild animals.

'Mister,' said a tiny red creature tugging at his leg. 'Please, mister, have you come from heaven?'

'Yeah, mister, are you an angel?' said another. The little creatures were bird mites and to them, Ted, who had suddenly appeared from nowhere, was a magical giant.

'I might be,' said Ted, looking down and hanging on for dear life as the bird swooped down into the garden again.

'Cor, can we worship you then, mister?' said the mites, all clamouring round Ted's knees.

'You can give me a present if you like,' said Ted, who was feeling peckish, which was quite funny considering he was sitting on a bird's back.

'We ain't got nuffink, mister,' said the mites.

'What, no food?' asked Ted.

'Only blackbird's blood.'

'Oh well,' sighed Ted. After all, he was a flea and although he had told his mother that he was a vegetarian, he knew that fleas live on blood.

The blackbird landed in a tree and as Ted curled up for a quiet afternoon sleep, it began singing at the top of its voice. Ted tried covering his ears with all six legs but it did no good. Another blackbird flew down and the two of them sang even louder. For the first time since he'd left the old rat, Ted wondered if it had been such a good idea.

There must be somewhere I can go, he thought to himself. *Somewhere I won't get jumped on or chased or deafened.*

Round the side of the house behind a great tangle of bushes there was a hole in the fence. Sometimes when the dog next door got fed up with her neat and tidy world where everything smelt of washing-up liquid and plastic, she would squeeze through the fence and come into the old garden.

Ted watched as she ambled around the edge of the flower beds sniffing every leaf as if it was a beautiful flower. In the dog's own garden the grass was so short that the lawn was no more than earth painted green. In Ted's garden, since the old lady had gone, the grass had grown rich and soft. It reached up to the dog's knees and she rolled over and over in it as if she were swimming through treacle.

Ted looked down. The dog was right underneath him on her back. Tiny black specks flashed in her brown fur, black flecks that looked like other fleas. Ted crawled to the tip of the blackbird's tail and jumped.

'Get out of it,' growled an angry voice.

'Yeah,' said another, 'or we'll pull your wings off.'

'Yeah, that's right,' said a third.

'I haven't got any wings,' Ted shouted. Something dark leapt out of the dog and landed in front of him. It was an angry flea with a mean look in its eye.

'It's all right lads,' he called. 'He's one of us.'

'We thought you was a mosquito,' said

another flea, coming out of the fur.

'Yeah, we've had a lot of trouble with mosquitos,' said the first flea. 'Coming here and trying to eat our dog.'

Ted told the two fleas, Dick and Rick, about the old rat in the drain and how he'd run away to find a better life. He told them about the mouse and the cat fleas and the red mites.

'They're rubbish, cat fleas,' said Dick.

'Not as rubbish as hedgehog fleas,' said Rick.

'Yes they are,' said Dick.

'Not.'

'You want a fight?'

'Yeah,' said Rick and the two fleas jumped on each other but before either of them could hit the other, the air was filled with a loud whining noise and a huge cloud of mosquitos came crashing down.

Fleas appeared from all parts of the dog, which was sitting by the house scratching itself. Its fur was full of struggling mosquitos all tangled up and swearing at the tops of their voices. The dog fleas charged into them with their legs flying.

Maybe I should've stayed on the blackbird, thought Ted, *or even on the old rat.*

As the battle went on all around him, he crept off to a quiet corner feeling quite homesick. Was there nowhere he could go to be happy?

The dog gave one great scratch and Ted went sailing through the air. Over and over he tumbled until he vanished into a world of total darkness. As he fell further away from the sunlight, sweet familiar awful smells drifted up towards him. He was back in his drain, and the stagnant water and the rat's bad breath that had once made him feel so ill now smelt warm and friendly. He looked down and far below the weak light shone on the lid of the rat's tin. As he raced by he reached out and grabbed its only whisker. He crawled into the rat's ear and lay there exhausted.

'You bone idle little scruffbag,' shouted a voice, knocking him out of bed.

'Hello, Mum,' said Ted. 'I've just had an awful dream.'

'I'll awful-dream you in a minute, my boy,' snapped his mother. His ears were aching and his head was ringing but Ted was smiling. He really was home again. And no matter how bad things sometimes seemed, he knew that it was where he wanted to stay forever.

The Rabbits

Right at the bottom of the garden behind the rusty car was where the rabbits lived. Their burrows peered out like black eyes between the twisted roots of trees that grew out of a bank of earth beneath the tall fence. Honeysuckle grew up from the roots, almost covering the fence and reaching its winding arms up into the branches. On the other side of the fence, past a thick forest of nettles and brambles, was a tow path that ran behind all the houses as it followed a canal into the middle of the town.

The almost endless honeycomb of tunnels that the rabbits lived in spread out from the fence like a huge underground city. It reached up the garden right to the brick walls of the cellars below the house. Through tiny cracks in the cement the rabbits could peer into the cellars and see the rats scurrying about through the old boxes and coal. In the other direction the warren went out under the canal, up on to the far bank where there was a field of wasteland covered in broken concrete and rubbish.

In the tunnels lived a rambling wild family of rabbits. They were not the shy secretive animals of children's stories who only come out at night to nibble the lettuces. These were loud fearless rabbits who jumped on the lettuces and ate the roses, rabbits who shouted and swore and sang rude songs and laughed and spat and threw stones into the pond.

On beautiful summer days when the garden was half asleep in the warm sunshine and the birds were singing softly in the wild strawberries and the whole world seemed to be standing still, they would go crashing through the grass, jumping on everyone's dreams. From their broken-down tunnels they spread noise and chaos to every corner of the garden. They went through the hedge, attacked next door's cat and bit the heads off the flowers.

'Go away,' mumbled the hedgehogs as they dozed under the geraniums.

'Rock and roll,' shouted the rabbits and they crashed through the undergrowth, snapping twigs and kicking up the molehills.

'Go away,' called Elsie the mole from her tunnel.

''Ere we go, 'ere we go, 'ere we go,' sang the rabbits as they ran laughing in a line round the lawn.

All afternoon, all evening and most of the night the racket would go on. There were rabbits creating chaos everywhere. When it was dark they tunnelled into other gardens and chewed all the heads off the marigolds and at midnight when the humans had just got into their beds and turned out the lights, they knocked the lids off the dustbins.

Only in the early mornings when the rabbits were sleeping was it peaceful in the garden. The sun came up, a big fuzzy circle in the mist that hung over the canal. Birds woke up, stretched their wings and slipped away through the trees. A hedgehog shuffled across the lawn making dark tracks in the white frost as it hurried back to its bed. From the rabbit warren came a chorus of loud snores punctuated with coughs and sneezes. From each tunnel little clouds of grey steam drifted across the garden carrying the smell of damp fur and mouldy grass.

As morning reached lunchtime sleepy rabbits would begin to emerge yawning into the daylight. They staggered through the bushes snorting and spitting and tripping over the dock leaves. By early afternoon they were banging and crashing away again as loud as the day before. At least once a week one of them fell into the pond and splashed around cursing until it managed to scramble out again.

'I've had enough of this,' said an old crow. 'I don't know what's got into them, but it's got to stop.'

'What can we do?' said Elsie the mole. 'If you say anything they just ignore you.'

'They weren't always like this,' said Ethel the old chicken. 'When I was young rabbits were sweet and fluffy. Now they're like wild animals.'

'They are wild animals,' said a rat. 'We all are.'

'I'm not,' said Ethel proudly. 'I'm domesticated.'

'Well, we've got to do something,' said the old crow.

The next morning while the rabbits lay asleep in their wildest dreams, the hedgehogs and the crows rolled big stones into the entrances of the burrows.

One by one they blocked them up until only the main tunnel was left open.

Then all the animals in the garden sat in a big semi-circle round the warren entrance and watched for the rabbits to come out. They slept late that day but the animals sat patiently waiting. Animals are not like humans, they don't get bored so quickly. Moles and slugs don't get bored at all.

At last the rabbits began to stir. From inside the blocked tunnels came the sounds of swearing and a lot of scrabbling commotion. At last some of them found the open entrance and came blundering out.

'Who's been blocking up our tunnels?' they shouted.

'We have,' said a huge crow, towering over the sleepy rabbits, the sun flashing on his large bill.

'Oh yeah,' said Ernie the rabbit, nervously. 'Well, you got no right.'

'Yeah,' said his mate Dave.

'We're fed up with all your noise,' said the crow.

'Oh yeah?' said Ernie.

'Yes,' said the crow, leaning right over the rabbit until his bill was touching its fur.

'Why do you have to rush round making such a

racket all the time?' asked the hedgehogs.

'Why can't you let us live in peace?' said the old chicken.

'Go and look in the other gardens,' said a blackbird. 'There's nothing there for us. You can see that and you can see that it's like that for miles and miles. Our garden is a special place, a place where no one comes to kill the weeds or the insects or to cut down the trees. It's a place where we can live together in peace, yet you insist on spoiling it all. Why can't you live quietly like the rest of us?'

Arthur, the oldest rabbit, came to the front and said, 'I'll tell you why.'

Arthur was the oldest animal in the garden. He was so old that none of the other animals could remember a time when he hadn't been there.

'I'll tell you why we shout and laugh and sing,' he said, and he told them the terrible story of what had happened.

'It's all right for you,' he said. 'Most of you never leave this garden from the day you are born until the day you die. Oh, yes, some of you birds fly up in the sky but from up there everything looks small and safe like a child's toy. But us rabbits go out into the world and come into contact with man. We have seen the awful things he can do and we have learnt to fear him.'

All the animals felt a sudden cold wind run through their hearts. They had never heard talk like that before. They all stared at the ground so no one else would see the fright in their eyes.

'Across the canal,' the old rabbit continued, 'across the wasteland, over the road hidden behind tall trees, there is an evil place. Two years ago some of us went there and we saw such terrifying things that we knew we could never be sweet and fluffy again.'

The sun was at its highest point in the blue summer sky. A haze of heat shimmered in the air yet all the animals were shivering. None of them knew what the rabbits had seen but they could tell it had been something almost too awful to talk about.

'Behind the evil place,' said Arthur, 'we found a row of dustbins and when, as animals do, we climbed into them to find food, we looked into the face of death. When we pushed off the lids the air was filled with the sweet smell of roses like a summer's day. But it was the middle of winter and there were no flowers there, just two blind rabbits with their eyes and bodies full of ladies' perfume. They were still alive so we led

42

them back across the river to the safety of the garden. And that is why we shout and swear and dance and sing, for all the other animals that are still in those awful places.'

The animals stood silent with an aching pain in their hearts. The young ones felt frightened and clung to their parents who were filled with a terrible anger.

'Isn't there anything we can do?' said the crow.

'No, nothing,' said Arthur.

'There must be something,' said a sparrow, but he knew there wasn't. They all knew there was nothing any animal could do. They knew that every single animal in the world survived only because man let them.

'That's why we shout and laugh,' said Arthur. 'We could all be dead tomorrow.'

'Couldn't you shout and laugh quietly?' said Ethel. She was an old hen and didn't really understand. The only human she had ever known had been the old lady who'd lived in the house and she'd always been really kind.

'We could eat the electric cables,' said the rats. 'That'd teach them.'

'You do that already,' said the crow. 'We could

43

build nests and block up their chimneys.'

'You do that already,' said the rats.

'Maybe if we all kept out of their way, they'd leave us alone,' said the old chicken.

'If only we could talk to them,' said a hedgehog.

'It wouldn't make any difference,' said Arthur. 'The only thing that will make men change is other men.' And he was right. Only the children growing up today can make tomorrow different.

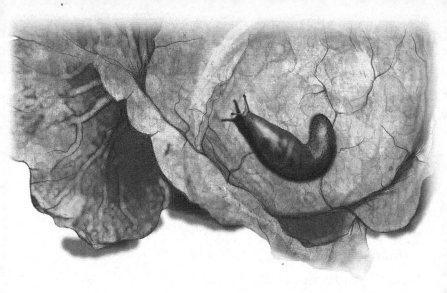

Bob the Slug

Behind the apple trees, past the overgrown pond, was the old vegetable garden. Once the earth had been neat and filled with rows of vegetables and fruit, but now nobody went there any more and the ground belonged to nature again.

Under an old brown cabbage that no one had wanted, hidden in a twilight world of soft green slime, lived Bob the slug. He was fat and black and sticky and shone like a piece of polished coal.

Every morning Bob and his family slithered out from their damp home and began to eat. They ate every green thing that lay in their path and each day

45

they had to slither a little bit further to find something new.

'One day,' said Bob, swallowing a daisy, 'we'll have eaten the whole world and there'll be nothing left to eat.'

'That's rubbish,' said his uncle Quentin.

'No, this is rubbish,' said Bob, biting into a mouldy plum.

'And you are dinner,' said Barry the hedgehog, eating them both and saving the world.

The Rats

After the old lady moved away, dampness spread through the empty house and the air grew tired waiting for someone to breathe it. The dampness brought cold, so even on a sunny day the house never grew warm. Behind the wallpaper the plaster began to crumble and behind the plaster tiny plants began to grow in the moisture that was creeping up the walls. And in the larder, sweet crumbs of food grew mould and turned to dust.

The house was filled with silence. The rats who lived in the cellars had been used to the sound of human footsteps moving above their heads. They were accustomed to the pitter-patter of the old dog shuffling from room to room. Now it was all quiet. The noises of taps and water running down pipes and drains, the muffled sound of the radio, had all stopped. Now there was absolutely nothing.

At first the rats hadn't noticed. The noises had been like the sound of cars out in the street that are there all the time so you aren't aware of them. They all felt uneasy but no one knew why. Then one day a young rat called Derek stopped chewing the electric cable and looked up at the silent ceiling.

'Listen,' he said.

'What?' said another rat. 'I can't hear anything.'

'Exactly,' said Derek.

Everyone stopped what they were doing and listened. The house was completely silent. Even the ticking of the kitchen clock had stopped.

'She's probably taken the dog for a walk,' said Derek's mum.

'But there's always some sort of noise,' said Derek.

'Nn nttthhhnnk mmms nggn mmmggyy,' said a voice from the shadows.

'For goodness sake, Neville,' snapped Derek's

mum. 'How many times have I told you not to talk with your mouth full?'

'Nnnnggyy, nnnmm.'

'NEVILLE!!!'

'Sorry, Mum.'

'Come here, and bring that sock.'

'What sock?'

'Neville, don't try and pull the wool over my eyes.'

'He's too busy pulling it over his own eyes,' sniggered Derek.

'I haven't got a sock,' said Neville.

'Well, what were you chewing then?' said their mum.

'Er, umm, a sausage,' lied Neville.

'Show me.'

'Er, I've eaten it all.'

'Well, in that case,' said his mother, 'you won't want any supper, will you?'

Neville started crying. In the dark corner his small shadowy shape could be seen shaking as his tears fell on to the floor. The sun came in through the cellar window and landed on his little wet feet. His mother went over and put her arms round him.

'It's all right,' she said, tickling his ears.

'I do try, Mum, honest,' he sobbed. 'I just can't stop myself.'

'But where do you keep getting them from? Socks don't grow on trees.'

Neville went silent and hung his head. He shuffled his feet and clung to his mother with his eyes tight shut.

'Well?'

'Squirrels,' said Neville, hiding in his mother's apron. He told her that when the squirrels next door ran along the clothes line to get to the bird table, some of the washing fell on to the lawn.

'Are there any knickers?' whispered Neville's brother, Trevor.

'TREVOR, I HEARD THAT!'

'Sorry, Mum.'

'And stop sniggering, you lot,' said the mother rat.

'Sorry, Mum,' they all chorused.

In the house, the larder was empty apart from an old jar of bottled fruit on the top shelf. It had been ages since they'd had a really good meal. They couldn't remember when they'd last had a lump of lard or some chocolate. The old lady had gone in the autumn so there had still been plenty to eat out in the garden. It was winter now and food was beginning to get scarce.

Derek peered cautiously round the larder door. The kitchen was deserted and smelt damp. He sniffed the air for clues but there was nothing, just the stale emptiness. In the old days there had been a warmth in the air, a soft mixture of sponge cakes and old lady's perfume and toffees, but now it was all gone. The other rats followed him nervously as he ran across the kitchen and out into the dark hall. Most of them had never been up into the house before and they felt frightened. Everywhere was so big. They were in a land of giants where the ceilings seemed as far away as the sky.

A thin layer of dust had settled on everything like dirty frost and the house was as silent as the middle of the night. Even the wheel in the electricity meter had stopped moving. Behind the front door was a tumbled pile of letters and newspapers.

'We'll eat those later,' said Derek as he led them up the stairs. Neville, who was little more than a baby, bounced up and down by the bottom step.

'I can't get up,' he cried.

'Well, go back down to the cellar,' said Derek.

'I'm frightened,' cried Neville.

'It's all right,' said Derek. 'Mum and Dad are down there.'

'Take me,' wailed Neville.

'Why?'

'I'm frightened of the light,' cried the baby rat.

Derek climbed down and led him through the bright kitchen into the larder. By the familiar hole that led down to the cellar, Neville clutched his big brother's fur and whispered: 'I wasn't really frightened.'

'I know you weren't,' smiled Derek.

'If there are any socks up there,' said Neville, feeling brave again, 'you'll save me one, won't you?'

'Of course,' said Derek. The baby rat ran down the tunnel into the cellar while Derek went back and led the others upstairs. Without him to lead them they had felt nervous and hadn't moved until he'd got back.

'It doesn't look as if there's much to eat up here,' said Derek, as they went from room to room.

All the furniture was still there but the old lady had taken everything else. The cupboards were bare and so were all the drawers apart from hairpins and talcum powder. They chewed their way into the mattresses but there was nothing there. They chewed their way into the armchairs but all they found was one boiled sweet covered in hairs and a lot of fluff. It was the same in every room, a squashed toffee here and a soggy crisp there, but nothing else. It wasn't until they got to the bathroom that they found any real food.

'It must be another larder,' said Derek. 'The old lady must have kept food up here in case she got hungry in the middle of the night.'

'Oh, wow, this is fantastic,' said Trevor as he nibbled all the bristles off the lavatory brush.

'I bet it's not as good as this,' said Derek, licking a hole right through the middle of the soap.

'No, this is the best,' said Derek's sister Tracy, sucking the flannel.

'You haven't tried this yet,' said someone else, chewing the lino round the toilet.

There were so many wonderful things to eat, it was difficult to know where to start. There were half-used tubes of toothpaste that tasted like strawberries, and roll-on deodorants that tasted like old armpits. Down the side of the bath there were bars of soap covered with delicious fluff and when Derek ate a hole in a laundry basket he found a sock for his baby brother. It was better than the socks Neville got from next door because it was very old and hadn't been in the washing machine. The old lady's bathroom was like a fancy restaurant with exotic meals from all over the world.

Over the next few months, the rats stripped the house. Even the oldest rat, Uncle Trubshaw, who had eaten nothing but oven scrapings all his life, was persuaded to come up from the cellar, and ate three hot-water bottles. Young Neville, with a bit of pushing and shoving, managed to get upstairs where he vanished into the laundry basket. When he came out a fortnight later he was incredibly fat and smelt very strange.

But all good things come to an end and after a few months there was nothing left but some unpleasant strips of green elastic and a shrivelled brown thing covered in hairy mould. Neville ate the elastic but nobody would touch the hairy thing.

'I'm sure I saw it move,' said Uncle Trubshaw and after that no one, not even Trevor, who had eaten the underneath of the toilet seat and one of those things you put in the water to make it go blue, would go near it.

They searched in the darkest corners, eating more and more indigestible things until there was nothing left they could get their teeth into. They ate the letters on the front doormat and then they ate the doormat. Neville tried to eat the telephone but cut his tongue on the '3' button. In the dining room there was wallpaper covered in strawberries but it tasted like two-hundred year old mildew. They cleared the tiniest crumbs from the kitchen and licked every last drop of spilt gravy until the whole room sparkled and looked cleaner than it had done for fifty years.

It was quite a long time since the old lady had left and the dampness that had begun in the cellar had now reached the roof. Any warmth that the sun put in through the windows was soaked up straight away and everywhere felt cold and clammy. Down in the cellar the rats huddled together in their nests and began to grow thin.

'Winter will be here again soon,' said Derek's mother. 'We should be warm and fat and ready for the snow, not feeling cold and hungry.'

They had spent so long inside the house that by the time they went back to the garden all the summer's fruits and berries had been taken by the other animals. To make matters worse, next door's cat had discovered their tunnel out of the cellar and spent hours waiting in front of it. It was only safe to go out late at night when the cat was indoors.

'Are we all here?' said Uncle Trubshaw.

'I think so,' said Derek. 'There should be twenty-three of us.'

'Twenty-two,' said his mother, coming in from the garden. 'I'm afraid next door's cat just got Trevor as he was trying to climb up the clothes line.'

'Oh, not Trevor,' wailed Neville.

'There, there,' said his mother. 'It's one of those

things. It happens to us rats all the time.'

'It's not that,' snivelled Neville.

'Well, what is it then?' said his mother, stroking his ears.

'I lent him three caterpillars last week and he hasn't paid me back yet,' said Neville.

Over the next couple of weeks things went from bad to worse. Humans came to the house, stomping round the bare floors in big shoes. Down in the cellar the rats crept in behind a loose brick and hid until the thunder above their heads moved away. The humans left but the rats were too frightened to go back upstairs except in the middle of the night. Besides, there was nothing up there for them now.

All they had to eat were a few soggy cardboard boxes and a packet of firelighters. Soon they were reduced to grubbing round in the garden for the other animals' leftovers. As the weather got colder and colder the rats got thinner and thinner. Next door's cat got Derek's dad and then three of his cousins. No matter how careful they were, the cat seemed to be one step ahead of them. As autumn turned to winter, the cat stayed indoors by the fire but by then there were only six rats left.

'It looks like you're the head of the family now, young Derek,' said Uncle Trubshaw.

'But you're the oldest, Uncle,' said Neville. 'It should be you.'

'Nay lad, I'm too old for all that,' said Uncle Trubshaw. He wasn't too old at all, he was too crafty. He knew that whoever was head of the family would have to sort out the problem of the cat and find them some food.

'Has anyone got any ideas?' said Derek.

'Me, me!' shouted Neville, jumping up and down.

'Well?' said the others.

'Why don't we go out into the street and –' he began, but Uncle Trubshaw went pale and shook his head.

'Out of the garden, you mean?' he said.

'Yes,' said Neville.

'Nay, lad,' said Uncle Trubshaw, 'I've never been out of this garden all my life and I'm not going to start now.'

'Have you got a better idea then?' said Derek.

'Aye, lad,' said the old rat, 'I have.'

'What?'

'We have to kill the cat.'

'Kill the cat?' said Derek. 'You must be mad. How on earth are we going to do that?'

'Aye, lad, we have to kill the cat,' continued Uncle Trubshaw, ignoring Derek's question. 'And when we've killed it, we can eat it.'

'Oh, that's revolting,' said Neville, sucking the insides out of a woodlouse.

'It's ridiculous,' said Derek, and the others agreed.

'Neville's right,' said Derek's mother. 'We have to leave here. While you were all out today there were more humans in the house.'

The next day Derek squeezed through the metal grating in the cellar floor and wriggled through the narrow pipe until he was in the drain under the street. The drain ran down the middle of the street and into an enormous tunnel as tall as a man. Derek could tell it was as tall as a man because just as he was about to jump down into it, a man went by carrying a torch.

There was a lot of wonderful food floating down the middle of tunnel but Derek ignored it and followed the man towards the centre of town. From the distance a thousand new and exciting smells rushed towards him. Other rats looked out of side drains as he passed. Some smiled and waved but most just looked and then disappeared.

'Psst,' said a voice as he passed. Derek ignored it and carried on after the man.

'Oi, Derek,' called the voice. Derek spun round and there was his little brother Trevor.

'Trevor!' he cried and ran over to him. Trevor was fat and bright-eyed and made Derek look even thinner and scruffier than he was.

'Mum said the cat got you,' said Derek.

'It did, but I dribbled on its tongue and it spat me out,' said Trevor. He led Derek down the narrow drains until they came to a round brick chamber. There were other rats there and they were all sleek and well fed.

'See that pipe,' said Trevor, pointing towards the top of the chamber. 'That leads up to the best Italian restaurant in the world and out the back are the best dustbins in the world.'

'There's enough for all of us,' said one of the other rats.

'Yes, no more toilet seats for me,' laughed Trevor.

Derek went back to the old house to fetch the

remains of his family. That night they went round the garden and said goodbye to all their friends and the following morning they left the old house forever. Even Uncle Trubshaw went with them. He moaned and complained and shook like a leaf but, although he was frightened of the outside world, he was even more frightened of being left alone.

'I'm only coming to make sure you get there safely,' he said. 'I'm not staying.'

He said it every day for the rest of the winter, but by the spring when he was fatter and fitter than he'd been for years, he made sure he only said it when there was no one to hear it.

Delilah the Spider

Delilah the spider sat very still in the corner of the window and waited. There was a fat bluebottle buzzing round the empty room and she knew if she waited long enough it would get caught in her web. A window is the best place for a spider's web because flies spend half their lives crashing into the glass. If they are outside they keep trying to get in, and if they are inside they keep trying to get out.

Insects are very stupid, thought Delilah, *but very tasty.*

A couple of mosquitos that she was saving for lunch wriggled in their silk prison and a bluetit hung on the window trying to peck them through the glass.

Birds are very stupid, too, thought Delilah, *but I wouldn't want to eat one.*

It was a beautiful clear autumn morning and when the sun had warmed the air Delilah had gone outside and laid three hundred and twenty eggs. They were wrapped in a soft yellow cocoon under the window sill, sheltered from the wind and rain. Next summer they would hatch and her babies would eat their way down the honeysuckle into the garden. Some of them would wriggle through the gap into the house and Delilah would probably eat them.

Babies are very stupid, she thought, *but very tender.*

When she had finished laying her eggs she had come back into the house and eaten her husband, Nigel.

Husbands are very stupid, she thought, *and very slow.*

The bluebottle flew round and round the bare light bulb and then dived straight into Delilah's web. It hung there caught by its leg and buzzed furiously. The louder it buzzed and wriggled the more it got caught and the more it got caught the louder it buzzed.

'Look, stupid fly, do you think you could keep the noise down?' snapped Delilah. 'I've got a terrible headache.'

She raced across the silken ladders and rolled the fly up into a parcel, but even when she had wrapped it tight it kept buzzing, so she ate it.

The mosquitos will keep till tomorrow, she thought.

There were other spiders in the room, but none on Delilah's window. She had chased them away into the dark corners where all they ever caught were dust mites and midges.

'Spiders are stupid,' said Delilah.

'You think everyone's stupid, don't you?' said a little brown spider called Norma from behind the skirting board.

'That's the only intelligent thing you've ever said,' replied Delilah.

'I think you're horrible,' said the little brown spider.

'Two intelligent remarks in one day,' sneered Delilah. 'If you're not careful your pathetic little brain will explode.'

Norma said nothing, not because her brain had

exploded, but because she was busy thinking of a way to get rid of Delilah.

It was bad enough now the house was empty, without Delilah making everyone's life a misery. There was no one to open the windows so hardly any flies came in. Without humans there were no smells of sticky jam and pies to attract them. What few bits of food the old lady had left had been eaten by the rats. It was all right for the spiders out in the garden, but as everyone knows there are thousands of spiders to every square yard and they certainly wouldn't make room for all the house spiders.

'It's not as if she's anything special like a tarantula,' said Norma. 'She's just a common house spider like the rest of us.'

'She's got the best place in the room and won't let any of us near it,' said Norma's neighbour Sybil.

'You don't have to tell me,' agreed Norma. 'Look what happened when Edwina tried to make a web at the other end of the window.'

'Well yes, I know,' said Sybil. 'She got eaten. I mean, Delilah even ate her own husband.'

'Something will have to be done,' said Norma with a firm stamp of several feet.

Something had to be done. That was obvious. The rest of the spiders, from the coal black shadows of the cellar to the draughty slates on the roof, all managed to live together with no trouble. Sometimes if a strange spider came too close to another's web it got eaten but that was perfectly natural and no one got upset about it. The spider doing the eating had a friendly word with its dinner and everyone knew where they were.

Delilah on the other hand had been nothing but trouble since the day she'd hatched. Within a week she had eaten all her brothers and sisters and her mother. She was as rude and vicious as she could be to everyone. If she couldn't eat them she swore at them. Something had to be done.

'Maybe we could set fire to her web while she's asleep,' suggested Sybil.

'Only humans can do that,' said Norma.

'Maybe we could get a wasp to sting her,' said Sybil.

'Do you want to go and ask one?' asked Norma. Sibyl didn't. She knew that wasps were one of the spiders' greatest enemies.

'Well, we've got to do something,' she said.

66

'It's all right,' said Norma. 'I have a plan.'

Norma's plan was the sort of plan that you make up as you go along. She knew what she wanted to do but she wasn't quite sure how to do it.

Every night under cover of darkness, all the spiders from the upstairs rooms built a huge web across the other side of the room from Delilah. Delilah could see it growing each day but she was far too important to take any interest in it. She was more concerned with her dinner. Since she had eaten the two mosquitos three days before she hadn't caught a single thing and was beginning to feel hungry. She slid down to the floor and stole a flea from Sybil's web and when Sybil protested she ate her.

'Not only are spiders stupid,' she said, 'they taste rotten.' The other spiders said nothing. Across the room they hid under their gigantic web and waited.

In the next room there was a broken window that had been covered up with cardboard. The spiders chewed at the sticky tape until the cardboard fell away. A blast of cold air blew into the room and ten minutes later two huge flies came through the hole and flew straight into the trap the spiders had woven behind it. That night the spiders carried the two flies up into the giant web and wrapped them up just enough to stop them escaping but not to stop them buzzing loudly.

Across the room Delilah woke up and heard the imprisoned flies. She could see them right in the middle of the web the stupid spiders had made and her mouth started watering. She scuttled round the wall and out along the silk rope towards the delicious feast. She was so hungry she felt quite dizzy and didn't notice the other spiders hiding at the corners of the web with their teeth in the threads. She reached the flies and as she did so the whole web went crashing to the ground.

Stupid spiders, thought Delilah as she ate the flies. *Can't even build a web properly.*

'Delilah, Delilah,' called a voice softly from above.

'Drop dead,' snarled Delilah.

'Are you enjoying your last meal?' called the voice.

'Last meal?' laughed Delilah. 'I'll eat you next, idiot.'

'I don't think so,' said the voice.

Delilah looked round. Through the tangle of the web she could see the white walls of the room. There was something strange about them, though. They had become all shiny like glass. Suddenly, she realised where she was but by then it was too late. Round and round she ran but it was no use.

'Bye, bye, Delilah,' called the voice. It was Norma, sitting on the bath tap, looking down into Delilah's prison.

George the Millipede

George the millipede had a terrible pain in one of his feet. It had been hurting him ever since he had tripped over a broken bottle in the front garden. For days he had slithered around with a peculiar wiggle. The other insects looked the other way when he went by so he wouldn't see them smiling.

'The trouble is,' he complained to anyone who would listen, 'I can't tell which foot it is.' With two hundred and forty feet to choose from it was hardly surprising. When you have toothache it doesn't always hurt in the right place. George's foot was the same. One minute he thought it was foot eighty-six on the left and the next it seemed to be foot one hundred and thirty-two on the right. Sometimes it was just behind his head and at others right down the far end.

'I know,' said his brother, Lionel. 'If I kick all your legs really hard, when I kick the sore one it will hurt more than the others and then we'll know which one it is.'

Millipedes are not very bright. They are even more stupid than sheep, so George thought it seemed like a good idea.

By the time Lionel had kicked a hundred of his legs George was beginning to wonder if it had been such a good idea after all. His eyes were watering and every part of him felt sore. Lionel was so exhausted he could hardly stand and was weaving about the lawn like a drunk worm.

'We can't give up now,' he said and stupid George agreed.

'Ow, ouch, ow, ouch,' he cried as Lionel worked his way down his side. And then at last he cried: 'OWWW!'

'That's it,' cried Lionel. 'That's the one.' He ran off to get a piece of dock leaf, but when he got back he had lost his place and had to kick George another twenty times until he found it again.

'Ohh, that feels good,' sighed George as he wriggled his bad foot into the dock leaf and limped home.

'Why didn't you just rub all your feet into the leaf?' said George's mother, who wasn't as stupid as her two sons. 'That would've cured it.'

George went bright red and spun round to catch his brother, but Lionel had slipped away across the dandelions.

Autumn

Between gold leaves
The butterfly
Folds its wings,
Soon to die.

Plants shrink back
Into the ground
As winter comes
Without a sound.

The days grow dark,
The air grows cold,
Nature sleeps
And time grows old.

Barry the Hedgehog

Across the lawn behind the old apple trees stood a wooden shed full of lawnmowers and broken deckchairs. Inside the shed there were cobwebs and dust and the air smelt of oily rags and dried grass. There was a wooden floor that groaned and creaked when anyone walked on it, and under the floor, snuggled into the warm dry earth, lived a family of hedgehogs.

For as long as anyone could remember they had lived there, sheltered from the wind and rain in soft dark nests of grass and newspapers.

Every spring, as the days grew brighter and warmer, they woke from their long sleep. They yawned and stretched and staggered out into the twilight to spend the summer out in the garden.

But now it was winter and time to rest. The leaves had fallen in golden piles and the shady corners where the hedgehogs had lived all summer were now open to the sky. Their hearts began to beat more slowly and their eyelids grew heavy. All round the garden they stopped what they were doing and lifted their faces to the chilly air. One by one they made their way back to the warm nest below the shed, where they curled up and fell into a deep sleep full of dreams of sunshine and soft slugs.

'Come on, Barry,' said a mother hedgehog to her young son. 'Time for bed.'

'Shan't,' said Barry.

'Come on now, there's a good boy.' But he just ignored her.

Barry had been nothing but trouble since the day he'd been born. His brothers and sisters had always behaved like hedgehogs should. They snuffled noisily round the garden eating slugs and earwigs and knocking milk bottles over. Barry kept squeezing through the hedge and stealing next door's cat food. And while everyone else slept the afternoons away under the rhubarb Barry rolled around collecting squashed plums on his prickles.

'I'm not tired,' he said.

'Don't be silly,' said his mother. 'It's half-past October. You must be tired.'

'Well, I'm not,' said Barry, jumping in a puddle. 'Anyway, I think hibernating's really silly.'

Barry's mother decided to leave him to it. When Barry got obstinate the best thing to do was to ignore him. She crawled under the shed and nuzzled into the nest. The air was filled with the smell of damp hedgehogs and a chorus of gentle snoring.

I'll fetch him later, she thought to herself, but in no time at all she was fast asleep.

'I'm staying awake, me,' said Barry to a sparrow, 'all winter.'

'Idiot,' said the sparrow and flew off.

Round the back of the shed was an overgrown pile of rubbish. At the bottom of the pile under brambles and old prams was a rusty kettle and it was there that Barry decided to live.

'I'm not going back under the shed with them,' he said, 'not ever.'

He collected some leaves and grass and pushed

them into the kettle. He chewed up the fat worms that had been hiding under the leaves and climbed into his new home.

'This is great,' he said to himself, 'better than that rotten shed.'

A crowd of starlings was gathering in the trees. Hundreds of them sat in long lines on the branches and across the roof of the house getting ready to go on holiday. The air was muddled up with their endless chattering.

'Oi,' shouted Barry, sticking his head out of his new home, 'come and see my house.'

'It's just an old kettle,' laughed the starlings.

'I'm staying awake all winter, me,' he shouted.

'Idiot,' chorused two thousand three hundred and forty-seven starlings and flew off to warm African gardens.

'Come back here and say that,' shouted Barry when they were out of sight.

The next few weeks were great. With all his

family asleep, there was no one to tell him what to do. There was no one to tell him when to get up, no one to tell him when to sleep and no one to tell him to be quiet. He rolled on his back in the mud, spat in the pond and shouted swear words he'd heard the rabbits use.

Fat and wicked, he sat in the little clearing in front of his house surrounded by young squirrels.

'Say another one,' squeaked the squirrels.

'BOTTOMS!' shouted Barry. All the squirrels sniggered and nudged each other.

'More, more,' they demanded. 'Show us how far you can spit.'

'Children!' shouted the adult squirrels from the trees above.

'Skinny rats!' Barry shouted after them as they all ran giggling after their parents.

The long grass was full of rotten apples that drew slugs from all over the garden. Barry got so fat he could hardly get into his kettle. The last of the golden leaves fell from the trees and the days grew shorter and darker. The other birds left the garden until there were only the sparrows and blackbirds left. Even the bluetits had gone next door to eat peanuts.

Through October the air held on to the last warmth of summer but in November it grew colder with mornings crisp and frosty. Barry was too excited with his adventures to notice the weather. When his breath came out in little clouds he climbed into his kettle and blew up the spout.

'Tea's ready,' he shouted.

'Idiot,' said a sparrow.

'You've got no sense of humour,' said Barry. 'That's your trouble.'

It wasn't until January that the adventure began to wear thin. The frost stayed all day now. Up at the empty house with no one to light the fire the windows were covered with ice like lace curtains. In the cellar the rats shivered and thought about moving to another home. The worms went deep into the ground and next door's cat was being fed in the house.

Barry shuffled around in the leaves finding fewer and fewer slugs. He began to lose weight and as he got thinner he lost his protection against the cold. At the bottom of his spines his fleas huddled together for warmth. He snuggled deep into his kettle and for the first time since autumn thought about his mother and his brothers and sisters. A lump came to his throat but his pride wouldn't let him go and curl up next to them under the warm shed.

'I'm staying awake all winter,' he said. But it was difficult to sound convincing with chattering teeth.

By February he was very thin and had a nasty cold that refused to go away. Every time the sun came out he thought that perhaps it was spring and that the others would soon come out from under the shed but the winter still had a long way to go and to prove it, it started to snow.

It began as he fell asleep and it snowed all night. Barry curled up as small as he could in his kettle but the cold went right through him. It crept down his spines like sharp needles. His paws had turned blue and hurt so much he could hardly move them. He knew now why hedgehogs hibernate. His tears ran cold down his face, turning to ice in the straw and making him even colder. His teeth chattered and his brain began to slide into a deep sleep.

With one great effort he pulled himself out of the kettle and went to look for the tunnel under the shed. But the snow had fallen so heavily that the entrance was buried and he couldn't find it. Round and round the shed he crawled getting weaker and weaker, until the greatest idea in the whole world seemed to be to curl up and go to sleep.

Sleep was wonderful. The snow grew warm as he faded away. He dreamt he was curled up in a nest of feathers with all his brothers and sisters. Then through the warmth, dark shapes appeared. Closer and closer they came, but Barry was so comfortable in the arms of death that he didn't see them.

'Hey, wake up,' said a voice.

'Come on,' said another, pushing him with a soft foot.

'Go away,' Barry heard himself mumble, but the voices kept pushing and poking him until he opened his eyes and unrolled.

Standing over him were Dave and Ernie, the two biggest rabbits in the garden. Barry suddenly felt afraid, but they were smiling down at him.

'Come on, young fellow. You can't sleep there. You'll be dead in no time at all,' said Dave.

'I can't find the way in,' said Barry, beginning to cry again.

'That's all right,' said Ernie. 'You come home with us.'

'But,' started Barry, remembering all the

warnings his mother had given him about the rabbits.

'You'll die if you stay out here,' said Dave.

The two rabbits led the little hedgehog through the snowdrifts towards the warmth and safety of their underground home. Barry's feet were chapped and split from the cold and left little spots of blood on the snow. It seemed to take forever to reach the bottom of the garden.

As they dived down the tunnel into the rabbits' home the smell of fresh summer grass rose up to greet them. Deeper and deeper they went into the warren. On all sides of them there were more tunnels leading off into snug rooms where groups of rabbits peered out as they passed.

'Watcha got there, Ernie?' shouted a laughing voice. 'A pin-cushion?'

'Nah, he's brought Hilda a bag of nails,' called another.

At last they took a sharp turn left and came to a stop. Barry was so out of breath from keeping up with the long-legged rabbits that he couldn't speak. He certainly wasn't cold any more.

Ernie's wife Hilda and six young rabbits sat in the corner eating grass.

'Look what we found out in the snow,' said Ernie.

'Poor little mite,' said Hilda. 'He looks half-starved.'

Barry had been too cold and frightened to think about it but he realised that he hadn't eaten anything for three days.

'Here, help yourself,' said the young rabbits, offering Barry their grass.

'I've never eaten grass,' said Barry. 'I don't think hedgehogs do.'

'Well, what do they eat?' asked Ernie.

'Slugs and worms and things like that.'

'Slugs?' chorused the young rabbits. 'How revolting.'

'Well yes, children,' said Hilda, 'it may seem revolting to us but it just so happens we're up to here with slugs and they're eating us out of house and home.'

'My goodness, you're right,' said Ernie. 'Wayne, Elvis, take our guest down to the larder.'

The two rabbits led Barry down deeper into the warren until they were far out under the river bed. They came to a huge cave piled high with grass and roots and leaves. Wherever he looked Barry could see thousands upon thousands of slugs. It was like a hundred Christmas dinners and three supermarkets rolled into one.

There were slugs of every size and colour from the tiny Mauve Mouthful to the wonderful succulent Brown Breakfast. There were slugs that Barry had heard about only in stories, like the Golden Gumdrop and the shining Great White Pudding. There were slugs that he had thought existed only in fairytales, like the exquisite Scarlet Slimebag that hedgehogs were supposed to have fought wars over. And lurking in the shadows like a vast beached whale was the gigantically massively hugely enormous legendary Black Banquet. It rolled across the grass swallowing half a lawn a day and blowing out clouds of foul smelling steam. There seemed to be an endless variety of slugs and they were all for Barry.

The rabbits couldn't bear to watch as he dived into a pile of grass and began to eat. One by one they turned green and left the room.

I don't know what they're so disgusted about, thought Barry. *At least I don't eat my food twice like they do.*

For the next three weeks Barry hardly left the larder. He ate and slept then ate some more and slept again. At first the young rabbits would hide in the tunnel giggling and daring each other to go and watch him eating but they all got used to it and he soon became friends with everyone.

'My mum and all the other animals say you're all crooks and dead common,' he said, 'but she's wrong.'

'We don't care,' said Ernie. 'Stops them bothering us.'

'She says you shout and swear all the time, but I think you're all great.'

'Well, we like to have a good time,' said Hilda.

'Rock and roll,' said Wayne.

'Yeah,' said Elvis.

March came and went and in early April Barry felt a breath of air from above ground tickle the back of his nose. Spring had arrived and was calling him.

Below the shed the other hedgehogs began to stir. Barry's mother rolled over and stretched. She reached out with her eyes still closed to where Barry should have been but the grass was cold and damp. At first she thought he might have got up early, but when she looked she could see that his bed hadn't been slept in at all.

She woke the others and they hurried out into the spring sunshine. Over a winter of hibernating they had grown thin and the sunlight blinded them after their long sleep of darkness.

'He's dead,' cried Barry's mother, 'I know he is. My poor little mite is frozen stiff and all alone.'

She snuffled around in the grass and bushes but there was no sign of him. She found his kettle but it was cold and empty.

'I blame myself,' said Barry's mother. 'I should never have left him.'

She raced round and round in circles looking for her son. There was no stopping her. The others tried to tell her she was wasting her time but she didn't hear them.

She ran in larger and larger circles until she was right out of the orchard and down near the bottom of the garden. She darted under bushes, looked deep into the pond, jumped over a rotten log and came crashing down on a big fat prickly mattress.

'Hello, Mum.'

'Barry?'

'Hello, Mum.'

'Barry, is it really you?'

'Yes, Mum.'

'I thought you were dead,' said his mother, hugging him the way only one hedgehog can hug another.

They went back to the shed and while all the others sat in a big circle he told them his story. It took two days to tell it because every time he started describing the wonderful slugs he had eaten everyone had to rush outside and find some food.

'Now then, young hedgehogs, just let that be a lesson to you all,' said a wise old grandfather.

'How do you mean, sir?' said Barry's little brother.

'Well, er, you tell them, Barry.'

'The moral of the story is that if you don't listen to your mother you could end up with lots of new friends and tons and tons of amazing slugs to eat.'

'BARRY!'

'Sorry, Mum.'

The Boy Next Door

Elsie the Mole had never felt so miserable in her life. She had a terrible headache and an awful cold and to make it worse she was in love with the boy next door who didn't even notice her.

She had caught the cold because she kept tunnelling up to next door's lawn in the middle of winter. Down in the tunnels where she lived with her mother it was damp and warm, but up above there was a thick frost on the grass and dark grey clouds full of snow.

'It's your own fault,' said her mother. 'Chasing round after that boy like that.'

'He doesn't even know I exist,' complained Elsie, sniffing loudly.

'Well, no nice mole would want someone who rushes around like you do,' said her mother.

Elsie's heart-throb was different from all the other moles. He didn't live in dark tunnels like the rest of them. He was a brave and fearless adventurer who spent most of his life tightrope walking across the garden. He had a brother who was just the same and together they performed an amazing double act high above next door's lawn. Sometimes one of them came down on to the lawn but Elsie was too nervous to speak and just peered out from the flower beds with her little heart full of love.

The reason Elsie had a headache was because of her cold. Moles who spend most of their lives in dark tunnels don't need to see and so they are nearly blind. They find their way round with their noses but because Elsie had a cold she couldn't smell anything. Usually she could pick up a worm's sweat twenty metres away, but now she couldn't even smell her own armpits and kept crashing into everything. Every time the tunnel went left or right, Elsie didn't. She went flying straight on into the wall and that was why she had a headache.

'Nobody loves me,' she wailed. 'I wish I were dead.'

'Why don't you just curl up in the nest and I'll bring you a nice hot slug?' suggested her mother, but Elsie just couldn't sit still. Every time she closed her eyes she saw the boy next door and had to go rushing off down the tunnels to find him.

Her eyes were streaming and her head was throbbing and even though she could hardly see past the end of her nose, she could tell that her hero was not there. She was heartbroken and waddled back to her nest to cry herself to sleep. He wasn't there the next day or the next. In fact, it was over a week before Elsie saw him again. By then she had decided that she would never love anyone again and would spend the rest of her life stamping on earwigs and kicking worms.

After a week her cold was getting better and she decided to go next door one last time. The winter sun shone softly through the cold air and there across the lawn, dark and mysterious, was her great love. He was lying asleep in the grass all black and dull like rich velvet.

It's now or never, thought Elsie and tiptoed shyly out from the lavender bushes. She ran across the lawn towards her sweetheart who lay in a dark blur beneath the clothes line. As she drew close, she tripped over a clothes peg and landed right on top of him.

'Oh, my darling!' she cried, flinging her stubby little paws around the dark frostbitten shape.

'Oi,' said Neville the rat, who had been hiding behind a concrete gnome, 'that's my sock. I saw it first.'

Ethel the Chicken

Behind the house, at the bottom of the overgrown garden, in a wooden box hidden under a bramble bush, lived a chicken called Ethel. On the side of the box was a label that said '1ST CLASS ORANGES'. Even though chickens are nearly as stupid as sheep, Ethel knew that she was not an orange.

'I am a chicken,' she said.

'Prove it,' said a young rat called Neville, who lived in a paper bag nest under the old house. He was only a child and had never seen an orange or a chicken before.

'Wow, a talking chicken!' shouted an ant, but no

one could hear her because she was very very small and before she could rush off and tell her four hundred and eighty brothers and sisters Ethel ate her.

'Listen, rat,' said Ethel, 'oranges are round and don't have feathers and don't lay eggs.'

'They might,' said Neville.

'You're a stupid little rat,' said Ethel, 'nearly as stupid as a sheep.' And she laid an egg.

'Is that an orange?' asked Neville.

'Of course not, it's an egg,' snapped Ethel.

'But it's round and got no feathers,' said Neville. Before Ethel could say anything else, Neville's mother came rushing down the lawn and grabbed him by the ear.

'How many times have I told you not to talk to strange fruit?' she said as she dragged him off.

Ethel settled back down on her nest and looked through the tall grass at the old house. It was a very long time since anyone had come out into the garden.

It's probably an hour, she thought to herself. The old lady who had lived in the house had gone away ages ago but chickens can't tell the time. She knew she hadn't been given any corn that morning but she'd had an enormous worm and a couple of lovely slugs for breakfast so she wasn't hungry.

When the old lady's nephew had come and taken all the furniture away they hadn't seen Ethel. They had come out into the back garden and folded up the deckchairs but Ethel had heard them talking about chicken and chips and had sat very still under the rhubarb until they'd gone. They'd closed the curtains, locked the doors and driven off in a red car.

Ethel felt that there was more to life than eating worms and slugs and laying eggs, but she didn't know what it was. She tried to think about it but chickens' brains aren't very good at thinking and every time she tried she fell asleep. As she sat there dozing away in the afternoon sunshine, young Neville came back.

'My mum says I've got to come and say sorry for being cheeky to you,' he said. Ethel said it was all right and that she was sure he was quite a good boy really.

'Can I be your friend?' asked Neville.

'Of course you can,' said the old hen, and they chatted about this and that for a while. Neville said his mum had been in a bad mood ever since the old lady had gone.

'We used to eat cake and toffees,' he explained,

'but now the house is empty we have to eat woodlice all the time.'

'I like woodlice,' said Ethel. But then, she had never eaten cake.

'I don't,' said Neville. 'All the bits stick in your teeth.'

'I haven't got teeth,' Ethel told him. 'I like the way their legs tickle as you swallow them.'

Neville looked a bit green at this and said he had to go and help his dad chew up some paper bags. Ethel told him to come and see her any time he felt like it. When he had gone she realised what the other thing was that she had been trying to think of. It was loneliness.

Since the old lady had gone, no one had come to see her. Every morning the old lady had come down the garden with a mug of corn and every morning she had tickled the top of Ethel's head and talked to her. Most of the time Ethel hadn't been able to understand what the old lady had been talking about but the words had always felt warm and comforting in her ears. Ethel was old herself and hardly ever laid an egg but the old lady had never seemed to mind.

It was only now that the young rat had started

to visit her that she realised how much she missed the old lady and how lonely she was. The hedgehogs who came and took the occasional egg she rolled out of her box were a miserable lot. You couldn't talk to them at all. When Ethel tried they just grunted a bit and shuffled off into the undergrowth. The other birds laughed at her because she was big and lumpy and couldn't fly and next door's cat just sneered at her. But then next door's cat sneered at everybody.

The next day young Neville came to see Ethel again. He told her about all sorts of wonderful things she had never heard of like skateboards and calculators. But when Ethel tried to talk about slugs, Neville grew restless and sat there fidgeting and sucking bits of woodlouse out of his teeth. Eventually he wandered off saying he had to help his dad again.

It was a lovely hot summer afternoon. Ethel sank into her nest, half asleep, and clucked softly to herself. Bright butterflies skipped in and out of the dandelion flowers whistling the latest tune. Ethel had never eaten a butterfly and wondered what they tasted like. She didn't know that they were just caterpillars with their best clothes on.

She could hear children playing in the garden

next door. She liked children. The old lady had brought some to see her once and they'd all tickled her feathers and cuddled her. It had made her feel very happy.

She thought about going next door to see the children but there was a big hedge and a tall fence all round the garden, far too tall for a fat old chicken to get over. At her age, it was all she could do to jump up on to the roof of her box. A diet of juicy worms and slugs had made her so fat that sometimes as she waddled around the lawn, she tripped over her own feet. It was no fun being old and even worse being lonely and old.

'You ought to try and get out a bit more,' said Neville's mum, when Ethel said she felt lonely. 'There's all sorts of things going on round the garden.'

'I'm too old for all that,' said Ethel. 'All I want is my old lady to come back.'

'You should go and meet the rabbits down by the apple trees,' Neville's mum went on, but there was no cheering Ethel up.

'I just want it to be like it used to be,' she said sadly.

The summer drifted lazily on. Neville came to

see Ethel less and less. He wanted to play with his friends, to chase squirrels and tease next door's cat, not listen to an old chicken talk about slugs. Neville's mother didn't come any more either, not now she had seven new children to look after. Ethel couldn't blame them, she knew she was boring. Sometimes just the simple effort of looking for worms seemed too much. In the good old days there had always been a magic in scratching away at the earth and jumping back, head to one side, to find some new treasure. Now everything seemed to have lost its taste. Grass, worms, daffodils or slugs, it was all the same. Only woodlice had any sweetness left and they seemed to run faster than they used to and be harder to catch.

The first leaves began to fall and a breath of cold crept into the garden. The children next door stopped playing outside and the air was filled with the thick smoke of autumn as everybody piled up the dying plants into smouldering bonfires. In Ethel's garden the dead flowers shrivelled up with no one to clear them away. They hung over like thin skeletons and in the mornings were stiff with frost. The golden leaves turned brown and collected in damp piles on the lawn. The days grew dark and short as winter covered the world. Ethel hid deep in her straw and tried to sleep. The slugs had finished and the worms had gone deeper into the earth. A few spiders still survived the cold and it was those that kept her going.

Rain came and broke up the old flowers and washed them into the ground. It washed the label off Ethel's box and dripped in through the cracks in the wood. It ran down her face so that if you had seen her you would have said you'd seen a chicken cry. The dampness crept into her bones and made them creak and her loneliness seemed to grow as dark as the winter nights.

She cheered up a bit when the snow came. It made the garden bright and clean. It covered her box with a thick coat that kept her warm and dry and it lasted for weeks. Neville began to visit her again and although Ethel knew he was only coming to get away from his baby brothers and sisters, she was glad to see him. He made a tunnel under the snow right across the lawn and sat shivering in front of Ethel's box telling her all his news.

'My dad's been eaten by next door's cat,' he said, through chattering teeth, 'and my brother Trevor.'

Ethel couldn't think of anything to say so she

tucked the young rat up in the straw next to her and clucked. It started to snow again, great big flakes that seemed to float around for ages before they landed.

'Why's it so cold?' said Neville, who had never seen a winter before.

'I don't know,' said Ethel. 'It always seems to be cold when it snows.'

'Is it going to be like this forever?' he asked.

'Oh no, it always goes away again,' said Ethel.

'What, back up in the sky?'

'I don't think so.'

'Well, where does it go?' asked Neville.

'I don't know,' she replied.

Neville's little sister, Tracy, popped up out of the tunnel and jumped up and down in front of them blowing out white puffs of cold breath.

'Mum says you've got to come home,' she squeaked. 'We've run out of paper bags.'

Neville climbed out of the warm and followed his little sister back down the tunnel. Ethel closed her eyes and dreamt of the old lady surrounded by sunshine and fresh grass.

The snow melted, more rain came and went and then one day the air seemed to be a little warmer. The sun grew bigger and stayed in the sky longer each day and opened new buds on the sleeping trees. Ethel got up and scratched about on the lawn. She found herself wandering further and further from her box into corners of the garden she had long forgotten. The rheumatism in her bones seemed to fade until she could no longer hear her joints creaking. She fluttered right up into an old apple tree and sat there feeling quite pleased with herself.

As she sat there fluffing her feathers out, one of the curtains at the back of the house opened and a man looked out. She kept very still. One by one all the curtains were opened, windows and doors too. Ethel kept so still that her legs went to sleep and she fell out of the tree. She lay in the grass but no one came. No one had seen her and after a while the man shut the doors and windows and went away.

Later on Neville slipped out of the shadows and jumped into Ethel's box.

'I'm not happy,' he said, sounding quite grown up. 'Humans and rats are not friends.'

'Don't be silly,' said Ethel. 'The old lady was wonderful.'

'She was old,' said Neville. 'She didn't know

we were there. Most people don't like us and try and kill us.'

'What on earth for?' asked Ethel.

'My mum says it's because we chew their slippers,' said Neville.

Ethel didn't know what slippers were and when Neville told her she got that horrid taste in her mouth you get when someone sucks a handkerchief. She said she was sure he was wrong and anyway perhaps the old lady was coming back. But she didn't. Over the next few weeks the man brought lots of people to the house but none of them was the old lady. Ethel sat quietly in her box and no one saw her. She knew in her heart that the young rat was probably right and she grew nervous at all the coming and going.

A few days later Neville and his mother came to say goodbye.

'We're going to live in this wonderful drain with my cousin Kevin,' said Neville, all excited. 'It goes right under the best restaurant in town. The rubbish is really great.'

Ethel felt very sad when they had gone. She even ignored a giant slug that slithered right in front of her box.

One day some people came to the house and stayed. They took down all the old grey curtains and put up new ones covered in big red flowers. At night the windows were filled with yellow light that poured out on to the lawn. New smells drifted down the garden, wonderful warm smells that Ethel had never experienced before. There was still no sign of the old lady. A man came out on Saturday and cut the grass. He passed right by Ethel hiding in the back of her box, but he never saw her.

Then as if by magic there were children in the garden. A boy and a girl running and laughing, climbing the trees and swinging from the branches. Round and round they ran throwing a big blue ball in the air. A big blue ball which bounced and rolled and rolled and rolled right up to Ethel's box.

'Look, look, look,' shouted the little girl to her brother. They reached out and tickled Ethel in exactly the right place. She shut her eyes and felt all her loneliness slip away.

The little girl tucked Ethel under her arm and carried her up to the house. The little boy ran beside her smiling and laughing.

Later on, the man gave Ethel a smart new box

with a label on the side that said 'BEST APPLES'.

'I am a chicken,' said Ethel to herself as she settled down into her wonderful new straw.

'And I shall call you Doris,' said the little girl as she poured her out a mug of corn.

BOOK 2

Waking Up

At the end of a quiet street at the edge of a large town, between tidy houses and tidy gardens, was a wild place. Once it had been a garden like those on either side with a neat lawn and straight rows of flowers, but some years before, the old lady who had lived there had moved away and since then the garden had become a dark and mysterious jungle. In the middle of this wild place was an empty house, called fourteen, that was slowly disappearing behind crawling bushes and overgrown trees.

As time passed, the grass grew taller burying the path from the front gate, the ivy crawled up the walls and slipped in through the broken windows. The trees wove new branches together and the garden became a closed and secret place.

In the jungle the honeysuckle filled the air with heavy dreams, and animals that had nowhere else to go made their homes in its welcoming branches and secret places. Moles and rats that had been driven from the tidy gardens all around took refuge there. Beyond the edge of the abandoned lawn under a thick bramble bush a chicken lived in an orange box, and up on the roof of the house crows had filled the chimneys with years of nests. Rabbits that could never find enough to eat anywhere else lived in a wild warren at the bottom of the garden beneath a crowded hedge. Beyond the hedge through brambles and giant hogweed taller than men a dusty towpath ran beside an old canal and across the canal was a desperate place of crumbling factories and fractured concrete.

The years passed and then one day as spring began to push the winter aside the old lady's nephew lifted away the broken gate and took his family to live in the neglected house.

Windows stiff with age were forced open and given new panes of glass and a coat of paint. The branches that had grown across them were chopped down and sunshine crept into the house for the first time in years. As the rooms grew warm again the dampness that had reached up to the highest ceilings was driven back into the earth.

In three quick weeks, the cobwebs were swept away, the holes that had let the rats in were filled up and the crows' nests were pushed out of the chimneys with stiff brushes.

When the chimneys were clear they lit fires in every room. The chopped down branches cracked as the flames ate through them and filled the air with sweet smelling smoke. The thin shoots of plants that had crept into the house behind the plaster shrivelled away and in a few days it was as if they had never been there. Once again the house was back in human hands.

Out in the garden the air was filled with nervous talk as the animals sat and waited. The homeless crows huddled in the tall trees and made everyone else miserable. Eventually they made new nests in the high branches but for months afterwards they complained to anyone who would listen.

'Just wait,' they said. 'When they've finished with the house, they'll come out here and kill the garden.'

The other animals said nothing because they were all frightened that what the crows were saying might be true.

'Of course, they'll wait until we've built new nests,' said the crows. 'They'll wait till we're all nicely settled in with fresh eggs ready to hatch, then they'll come out and chop everything down until it's as flat and dead as all the other gardens.'

It looked as though the crows were right, for as spring turned into early summer the man bought a bright red lawnmower and attacked the back garden. The machine flew over the grass like an eagle, tearing it to pieces as it passed. The green tunnels that the mice had made over the years vanished in a minute, leaving a wide open yellow space that was unsafe to cross. From her box under the bush Ethel the chicken sat very still and watched him go by. From the tops of the trees the crows looked down, too scared of the man to go and pick up the worms he had disturbed. All the terrible things they had predicted were coming true.

Every weekend the family pulled out the weeds that had grown around the house and swept up the dead leaves. They cut back the ivy until it was no taller than a dog and piled everything up into a huge bonfire in the old vegetable garden.

In the evenings as the days grew longer the man

sat in an armchair by the French windows, gazed out across the tidy lawn at the dense undergrowth beyond and fell asleep. Sometimes he would wake up just as the light was fading away and see the rabbits and hedgehogs moving softly in the shadows. Sometimes he would see the blackbirds hopping across the grass and other birds flying in from all around to roost in the tall trees. Maybe something told him that if he cut everything down they would all go away, or maybe he was just lazy, but as the summer grew warmer his enthusiasm for gardening grew less and less.

The animals grew more and more restless. They knew the people would chop everything down. That's what people did, they only had to look at every other garden to see that. But the family finished playing with their bonfire and then left everything alone. Some of the smaller more nervous animals like the voles and the shrews moved out into the narrow strip of wasteland by the canal, but for most of them there was nowhere else to go and they just had to watch and wait.

'They're just biding their time,' said the crows.

'What for?' asked Ethel the chicken, but no one knew.

And then something happened that made the family make up its mind once and for all.

In the next house there were two miserable people who complained all day long. As she complained about the sunshine, he complained about the cold. When he complained about the noise, she said it was too quiet. They complained to each other about everything and when they could no longer stand to listen to their own voices, they wrote and complained to the newspapers. They hated everything and everyone but most of all they hated the overgrown garden next door that dropped leaves onto their tidy lawn and cut out the daylight and threatened them with its untamed life.

'My wife wants you to cut down the trees by our fence,' said the nervous man. He stood shuffling from foot to foot on the doorstep while his wife hid behind her plastic curtains.

'Why?' said the man.

'She says they drop leaves on her flower beds,' said the nervous man.

'That's all right,' said the woman. 'You can keep them, we've got loads more.' In the next room their two children laughed and the miserable man went away. His miserable wife came to the door and she complained about the squirrels and the hedgehogs and the rabbits and the mice.

'I didn't even know we had squirrels,' said the man. The miserable woman went away and wrote a letter to the town hall who lost it in a wastepaper basket with the eighty-six others she had sent them. Seven times they went back to fourteen to complain and the last time they said they'd get the police. The family laughed and thanked them for saving them so much work, because whatever they had been planning to do in the garden they certainly weren't going to now.

'Anyone can have a rotary clothes dryer in their garden,' said the woman after the miserable couple had gone back to their net curtains and pampered cat, 'but only special people get squirrels and hedgehogs.'

And they built a bird table and put out nesting boxes for the bluetits.

The family's two children tunnelled down the garden, crawling like voles through the undergrowth and above a clearing of soft grass in the branches of a wide oak tree they built a tree house. They lay flat on their stomachs and looked down into the overgrown pond as the moorhens led their chicks away through the ferns to the canal.

Nearly Spring

Long nights as black as sleep,
Short days bleached grey with cold,
The sun hangs weak as water
In a sky grown flat and old.

In oak trees stripped and brittle,
Round shouldered sparrows sleep.
Through grasses bent and broken,
Cold slow creatures creep.

As every night grows shorter
The air turns soft and warm.
Nature cracks her frozen teeth,
Spits frost across the lawn.

Long days as soft as smiles,
Short nights that rest the soul,
The moon hangs pale as violets
In a sky of speckled coal.

Albert the Bat

In the dark loft at the top of the house, in the darkest corner where the slates met the wall, lived a family of bats. They had lived there for as long as anyone could remember. Long before the old lady had left the house and even before she had been born, there had been bats under the roof. They were there even when Queen Victoria had been on the throne. They were an old and noble family treated with great respect by all the other animals apart from the moths who had been their supper for over a hundred years.

At one time there had been bats in every attic down the street but now they had all gone except for this one family. One by one they had been driven out by loft conversions or killed by woodworm spray. Only under this roof, untouched and quiet like the garden below, was there any safety.

The last few winters had been long and cold. With no fires in the empty house the air in the loft was cold and damp and the bats had hibernated right up to the end of spring. Now there were people in the house and warmth rising from the rooms below soaked through the chimneys next to the bats' roost. It was March outside but under the roof it felt like the beginning of summer. One by one the sleeping bats woke up. The crumbling plaster between the rafters was full of drowsy butterflies who had also woken up too early and the bats lived on them until the evenings grew warm enough to go outside.

The young bats who had never hibernated before woke up feeling very strange and unable to understand how they had got so much older in their sleep. They fluttered around in confusion, falling on to the tops of the ceilings and crawling around in the dust. Their mothers swooped and dived above them coaxing them back into the air.

'If you stay like that with your feet on the

ground,' they said, 'the blood will rush to your feet and you'll get dizzy.'

Of all the bats in the attic the oldest was Albert. He was twenty-three years old and he was having trouble with his radar.

'I keep hearing voices in my head,' he said. 'Far away voices that sound like men.'

'What are they saying?' asked the others.

'I don't know,' said Albert. 'They're too far away to tell.'

'Perhaps they're voices from the other side,' said Flossie who believed in that sort of thing.

'The other side of what?' asked a young bat called Ryan.

'You know,' said Flossie, going all mysterious, 'voices from beyond.'

'Beyond what?' said Ryan, trying to keep a straight face which can be difficult for a bat.

'Ryan,' called his mother, 'stop being cheeky to your Auntie Flossie.'

'I don't care where they're coming from,' said Albert. 'I want them to stop.'

'You're probably tired,' said Ryan's mother. 'You probably just need a rest.'

'A rest, a rest?' said Albert. 'We've been hibernating all winter, how could I need a rest?'

The trouble was that the voices in his head were interfering with his radar and it's radar that bats use to find their food. Every time Albert flew out into the garden to catch moths all he could hear was blurred noises like a ventriloquist's dummy shut in a suitcase.

The voices weren't always there. As the night moved on they grew less and less and in the early hours before dawn they usually went away altogether. By then of course the other bats had caught the biggest moths and Albert had to make do with the stragglers that were still throwing themselves at the streetlight outside the house. They flung themselves at the brightly lit glass and as they fell unconscious to the ground Albert swooped and caught them before the old cat waiting at the bottom of the lamppost could get them.

'I'm fed up always getting my food broken,' he said. 'They crash into the light and get all dented.'

'It could be worse,' said Ryan's mother. 'You could be a vampire bat and have to suck blood out of people's necks.'

'Or cow's bu–' Ryan started to say, but his mother stopped him.

The nights grew shorter and warmer and the voices in Albert's head grew louder. He still couldn't make out what they were saying but they were definitely getting stronger. All the other male bats had gone off to spend the summer in hollow trees and the deserted factories across the canal. The canal itself was a wonderful place for food. At dusk it was alive with insects that drove men away and drew bats in.

The loft was full of new born babies now and everyone was too busy looking after them to bother with Albert's problems. Twice a night all the mothers flew off to feed leaving him alone with hundreds of tiny twittering creatures. He couldn't decide which was worse, the noise they made or the noise in his head.

And then one night one of the voices grew so loud that he understood what it was saying.

'Are you there?' it said. It was a man and he sounded in a bad mood.

'Err, yes, I'm here,' said Albert nervously.

'You'll have to speak louder than that,' said

Flossie, 'They'll never hear you on the other side.' And they hadn't, for a few seconds later they called again.

'Oi mate, are you there?' it said.

'Oi mate?' said Albert. 'They're not very cultured, these spirits of yours, are they?'

'Answer it, quickly,' said Flossie, 'and shout this time.'

'HELLO?' shouted Albert, but they still couldn't hear him, because a few seconds later the voice called out again and filled Albert's head up with a lot of very rude words, most of which he had never heard before. He repeated them to Flossie who looked shocked and then said in a low whisper: 'I think they must be from down there.'

'Down where?' said Ryan.

'Down there,' repeated Flossie. 'You know, H-E-L-L.'

'Ooerr,' said Ryan.

Albert thought that all this talk about spirits and ghosts was a load of rubbish but he went very quiet and put his wings over his head. He tried to sleep but the voices wouldn't go away. All night they shouted at him and all night he ignored them. And then, just before dawn, the man stopped calling him and a woman's voice came into his head and she spoke to him by name.

'Bert,' she said, 'can you go to the Golf Club?'

'They want me to go to the Golf Club,' he said to Flossie.

'Well then, we'd better go, hadn't we,' Flossie replied and together they flew off into the sunrise. As they coasted over the tall trees and out of the garden the voice said: 'You better fly, you should've been there hours ago.'

'Well, we're hardly going to walk, are we?' said Albert.

When they reached the Golf Club, the two bats slipped up under the eaves of the clubhouse and slept. That night when they woke up Albert could hear nothing but wonderful clear silence and the soft noises of moths fluttering in the dark. Nor did he ever hear the voices in his head again except on Saturday nights when the radio taxis came to collect the golfers at closing time.

Four Bluetits

Two bluetits were sitting on a branch looking across the garden at a wooden nesting box nailed to the back of the house. Two other bluetits were hopping in and out of the box.

'Look at it,' said Max. 'I ask you. Modern homes.'

'I know,' agreed Jim. 'Plywood rubbish.'

'I mean, that's not a home, not a proper home you'd want to bring kids into, is it?' said Max. 'I mean, where are the nice knot holes and the rough bark crawling with all those tasty insects? Where are the body lice hiding in the cracks?'

'Yeah, it's just a bloomin' box,' said Jim.

'I tell you what,' Max continued, 'you put a load of grass and fluff in there, six eggs and the wife, and the bottom'll fall out of it. You'll see.'

'I know,' agreed Jim, 'but you can't tell them, can you?'

'Tell them, tell them? I should think not. I've not had a minute's peace since those boxes were put up.'

'The man's put a couple of big ones up over there, see?' said Jim. 'And a pair of starlings were straight in there before he'd even put his hammer away.'

'Well, what do you expect with starlings,' laughed Max. 'Thick as two short planks.'

The two birds laughed so much they almost fell off their twig. Max hung upside down and said, 'Here, how many starlings does it take to change a light bulb?'

'Dunno?'

'None, because they're all too thick.'

The two birds began laughing so much that this time they did fall out of the tree.

'Well, you won't get me into one of them,' said Jim as they flew over to a new bird feeder. 'Not in a million years.'

'Isn't it wonderful?' said Trixie, hopping out of the nesting box. 'A home of our own.'

'Gorgeous,' said Katie.

'Every modern convenience you could wish for,' said Trixie. 'Just look at that entrance hole, a perfect circle.'

'I envy you, I really do,' agreed Katie.

'And would you look at that perch. Go on, have a hop on it.'

'Ooh, isn't it fabulous,' said Katie, 'just the right size for your feet.'

'I know. And look at that lovely bit of felt on the top and those shiny little nails. That's quality that is.'

'And what about Jim?' asked Katie. 'What does he think?'

'Think, think? He doesn't think,' said Trixie. 'He's too busy hanging round that new bird feeder all day showing off to the sparrows to think.'

'My Max won't have one,' said Katie. 'He says they'll fall to bits.'

'They'll outlast the pair of them,' laughed Trixie. 'My Jim's so fat from eating peanuts I shouldn't think he could even get in the door.'

'My old man's the same.'

'So fat they'll have to live in that big box over there,' laughed Trixie.

'Yeah, next to the stupid starlings,' roared Katie and they both shook so much with laughter that the nesting box fell off its hook onto the lawn.

'See,' said Max, looking down at the pieces of broken wood on the grass. 'I told you they weren't safe.'

DorisEthel

DorisEthel sat in her apple box looking across the lawn at the house. The sun was warm on her feathers, the air was soft and still and the old chicken soon fell asleep. As she slept she dreamt of days gone by when she had been young and there had been other chickens in the garden.

They had all lived in a smart hut with three nesting boxes and the garden had been full of fresh earth to scrape about in. In her dream there were worms as fat as carrots and there were fluffy yellow chicks round her feet looking up at her with love and admiration. And she dreamt of Eric. What a wonderful cockerel he had been, so tall and bossy and with such lovely tail feathers. DorisEthel could still remember how proud she had felt every morning when he had flown onto the shed roof and crowed his head off. She could remember too, running away just before next door's upstairs window opened and the bucketful of water came flying out. Eric may have been big and beautiful but he had also been very, very stupid. Every morning, just after his third cock-a-doodle-doo, he had been soaked to the skin. The window opened, Eric looked up at the noise and got the water right in his face.

'I'm going down the bottom of the garden tomorrow,' he used to say, but he always forgot and DorisEthel didn't see why she should remind him.

When DorisEthel woke up she was broody. It was a terrible fidgety feeling that she hadn't felt for years and years and no matter what she did she couldn't settle down. She wandered round the garden to all her favourite places, but none of them seemed quite right.

The old hut where all the chickens had lived was broken down now. She hopped up inside it and looked in the nesting boxes. They were all full of weeds and the wooden sides were broken and rotting away. There were holes in the roof and a small tree growing up through the floor. In a few more years there would be nothing left except a pile of compost and some rusty nails.

'I'm too old to lay an egg now,' she said to herself. 'Anyway, Eric's not here any more.'

The air was filled with the hum of early summer. Flies hovered above the bright grass and a lazy robin hopped through the branches of a nearby bush. On the lawn the children were lying in the grass reading. Their mother was asleep in a deckchair. She had been knitting a cardigan but as the sun had climbed higher in the sky and the day had grown warmer she had nodded off.

I wonder if she's dreaming of eggs, DorisEthel thought to herself.

As she walked past the children, DorisEthel saw a big round egg. It was powder blue and lying in a soft fluffy nest in a basket. No one was sitting on it or even paying it any attention so she climbed up and settled herself down. She closed her eyes and was soon fast asleep.

'Hey, chicken,' said a loud voice. It was the

children's mother and she was poking DorisEthel with her finger. The children were standing beside her laughing and pointing.

'Hey, chicken,' said the woman, 'get off my knitting.' She picked up the old chicken and put her down on the grass. The children tickled the top of her head but it didn't seem to feel as good as it usually did and she wandered off into the bushes clucking to herself. A big black slug was eating its way across a dock leaf right in front of her but DorisEthel just didn't feel hungry.

'I don't want much out of life,' she muttered to herself as she drifted restlessly round the garden. 'Just a dry box, some soft straw and something to hatch. It isn't much to ask.'

She walked past the rabbits and under the tall trees complaining softly to herself. The other animals called out good mornings as she went by but she didn't seem to notice any of them. She dragged her feet in the earth, looked out across the canal and sighed deeply.

'What's the matter with the old chicken?' they asked, but no one knew.

'I just want an egg to sit on,' said DorisEthel.

'An egg?' said a rabbit. 'You're too old for that sort of thing.'

'Yes,' agreed another. 'You should be enjoying your retirement.'

'Exactly,' said a third. 'You don't want to be thinking about children at your age.'

'It's all very well saying that,' said DorisEthel, 'but you're not a chicken. That's what we do, sit on eggs. That's what we're for.'

As the days went by and the summer grew fuller, DorisEthel got more and more miserable. All around her the other animals had children. Baby rabbits peered out from the safety of their burrow as she went by. Above her in the trees the nests were full of hatching eggs. In curled up nettle leaves tiny new spiders ate their way to the outside world and in the pond tadpoles wriggled in the sunlight. Even in the old overgrown car by the apple trees there was a nest of young sparrows. It seemed as if the whole world had babies except her.

No one could say anything to get the old chicken out of her mood. As the days went by and the summer grew fuller, she got worse and worse. If she went near anything that was in the slightest bit round she sat on it and tried to hatch it. The garden was soon full of squashed toadstools and polished stones. Whenever she found some dry grass and a few twigs she scraped them up into a nest and sat in the middle of it with her eyes shut. One day as she ambled across the lawn Elsie the mole popped up from her tunnels and before she could burrow down again DorisEthel sat on her.

'I could have sworn it was morning,' said Elsie as she opened her eyes in total darkness. She thought the sky had fallen down on top of her but when she realised that the sky smelt of damp chicken she understood what was happening.

'If you don't get off me this minute,' she shouted, 'I'll bite you.'

'I thought you were an egg,' said DorisEthel as she stood up. 'Sorry.'

'Do I look like an egg?' said Elsie.

'Some days everything looks like an egg,' said DorisEthel. 'And today's one of those days.'

'Stupid chicken,' said Elsie and dived back into her tunnel. She had smelt a big worm thirty feet away and wanted to catch it before it got away.

DorisEthel wandered aimlessly down to the pond and stood ankle deep in the mud at its edge.

For half an hour she just stood there staring into the water. Little creatures wriggled between her toes in the puddle but she didn't notice them.

'Excuse me, mister,' said a voice beside her.

'What?' said DorisEthel, too depressed to bother telling the owner of the voice that she was a mrs not a mister.

'Is that your mud or can anyone have a go?'

DorisEthel looked down and saw a huge round toad sitting on a clump of grass staring at her. She dragged her feet out of the mud and paddled off into the undergrowth.

'Help yourself, warty,' she said.

'Ooh, someone got out of bed on the wrong side this morning, didn't they?' said the toad and flung himself into the puddle.

The next morning DorisEthel felt a little better. The children brought her mug of corn before they went off to school and when they tickled her on the head it nearly felt wonderful again. But the broody feeling was still there. Every time she shut her eyes she saw fluffy yellow chicks running round her legs.

'Cuckoos are always on the lookout for somewhere to lay their eggs,' said one of the rabbits.

'Why don't you have a word with them? Maybe they'd lay one in your box.'

'What's a cuckoo?' said DorisEthel and the rabbit told her.

'That's awful,' said the old chicken. 'I don't want some horrible bird kicking all my babies out of their nest.'

'You haven't got any babies,' said the rabbit.

'I will have,' said DorisEthel, 'when Eric comes back.'

The rabbit started to say, 'Eric was a casserole years ago,' but she stopped herself and said, 'Oh yes, well, I hadn't thought of that.'

'Well, I'm going back to my box in case Eric comes back while I'm out,' said DorisEthel and walked off. When she got to the lawn she remembered about Eric.

'What a stupid old chicken I am,' she said to herself.

It was Sunday afternoon. The man came out of the house, uncovered a small hole at one side of the lawn, dropped a golf ball at the other and swiped it with a golf club. The ball rolled across the grass and after another couple of taps fell into the hole. He took another golf ball out of his pocket and sent it down the hole after the first one. Over and over again he took the two balls to one side of the lawn and knocked them back into the hole. Two sparrows were sitting in a tree watching him.

'What do you think he's doing?' said the first sparrow.

'I haven't the faintest idea,' said the second, 'but I'd be suprised if they hatch out after the bashing he's given them.'

'Absolutely,' said the first sparrow. 'The shells must be as hard as concrete.'

'Yeah,' said the second, 'and whoever's inside them must have a terrible headache.'

The constant clattering of the golf balls finally woke DorisEthel up. She watched the man put an egg on the grass and bash it with a bent stick. The egg flew across the lawn and vanished and then the man did it again. DorisEthel couldn't believe it. The man had been so kind to her. He'd given her a smart new box to live in and every day his children brought her food.

Yet here he was killing baby chickens.

DorisEthel climbed out of her box and ran onto the lawn squawking loudly. As a golf ball rolled past her she threw herself on top of it. The man walked over and squatted down beside her laughing.

'What are you doing, chicken?' he said with a smile. Animals can't understand what humans say any more than humans can understand animals so DorisEthel just sat there glaring at him.

'Stay there,' said the man, 'I'm going to get my camera.'

He got up and went into the house. The minute he was out of sight DorisEthel stood up and pushed and shoved the golf ball until it was hidden in the long grass. By the time the man got back with his camera she had sunk down on top of it almost out of sight.

'Doris,' called the man, 'where are you?'

He went back into the house to get his family to help him find DorisEthel and while he was gone the old chicken rolled the other ball into her nest.

'An egg,' she murmured to herself, 'and another egg.'

'She's not in here,' said the children, looking in her apple box.

'Five eggs,' whispered DorisEthel who couldn't count.

'She's not in the shed either,' said the woman.

Seven eggs, thought DorisEthel.

At last they found her. She sank down as flat as she could but the man slid his hand underneath her and found the two golf balls. But he didn't take them away because he knew what DorisEthel wanted and the next day he got planks of wood and a roll of felt and mended the old hen house. When it was finished and tight against the wind and rain he filled it with fresh straw and five eggs from a chicken farm. Then he sat DorisEthel in her new nest and gave her a bowl of rice pudding, which was her favourite food.

For almost three weeks DorisEthel sat on the eggs. On good days the man left the hen house door open and DorisEthel dozed in the sunshine. In the middle of the day when the sun was at its hottest she climbed off the nest and went outside to stretch her legs and eat a few slugs. On wet days she sank down into the warm straw and listened to the summer rain dancing on the roof. Inside the eggs life began to stir and DorisEthel could feel the chicks tapping at the shells.

At last the waiting was over and one by one the eggs broke open and once again DorisEthel had fluffy yellow chicks round her feet, looking up at her with love and admiration. And once again she felt loved and important.

'We'll have to find names for them all,' said the little girl.

'Which ones are boys and which ones are girls?' said her brother but no one knew.

'Oh well,' said the girl, 'we'll just have to call them all Doris.'

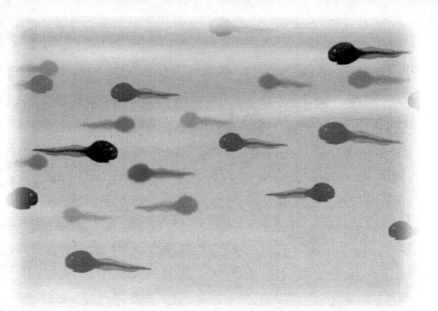

Brenda the Tadpole

It was midday and the sky was blue from side to side. The sun shone down into the pond through a colander of leaves. Two moorhens swam around, leaving ripples in the water that carried the light into dark corners at the water's edge. A frog blinked and slipped into the water with a soft splash. Dragonflies, woken by the warmth, flew backwards and forwards along their territories meeting each other with a fierce clattering of wings before flying on again. Birds came to the edge of the pool to drink and on its surface pondskaters dented the water as they hunted for food.

Below the water was another world, a world

hardly touched by wind or rain, a complete universe of tiny jungles and fearsome creatures. Great diving beetles hunted through the roots of waterlilies like lions. Newts paddled through the pondweed like tiny dinosaurs in slow motion, and in a shallow sunlit corner, new tadpoles hung on clouds of soft green slime.

'Do you like being a tadpole?' said a young tadpole called Susan.

'How do you mean?' said one of her sisters.

'You know,' said Susan, 'would you rather be a tadpole or something else?'

'Like what?'

'I dunno,' said Susan.

'A filing cabinet,' said a tadpole called Doreen.

'What's a filing cabinet?' said Susan.

'It's that brown rusty thing down there in the mud,' said Doreen.

'You don't half talk a load of rubbish, you lot,' said a tadpole called Brenda.

'Oh yes,' said Susan. 'And what amazingly important things have you got to talk about then?'

'Well, what about green slime?' said Brenda. 'That's important.'

'Go on then,' sneered Doreen, 'talk about green slime.'

'Well, it's nice isn't it?' said Brenda.

'Is that it?' said Susan.

'Er, yes,' said Brenda.

'Great,' said Susan. 'That's really important. Green slime's nice. That's brilliant.'

'Well, what about our mummy,' said Brenda. 'Why haven't we got a mummy?'

Doreen and Susan and the other tadpoles looked awkward and confused. It was midday and the sun was as high as it could be in the sky. Bright light shone down into the pond, in some places reaching right down to the mud at the bottom. All the tadpoles wriggled nervously in the sun's warmth.

'Of course we've got a mummy,' said Susan. 'We wouldn't be here if we hadn't had a mummy.'

'The waterlilies haven't got a mummy,' said Doreen.

'They don't count,' said Susan. 'They're plants.'

'Maybe that's what we are,' said Doreen. 'Plants.'

'Don't be ridiculous,' said Brenda. 'We're animals and as far as I can see, we haven't got a mummy.'

'Or a daddy,' said Doreen.

'We must have,' said Susan.

'All right,' said Brenda, 'where is she?'

'Maybe she's not in the pond,' said Susan.

'She'd have to be,' said Brenda. 'We can't leave the water, can we?'

The others agreed she was right and so a search was organised. All eighty-seven tadpoles swam round the pond searching for the giant tadpole that would be their mother. An hour later the seventy-four that hadn't been eaten gathered together in the cloud of green slime.

'Well,' said Brenda, 'has anyone seen our mummy?'

'No,' said everyone.

'Me neither,' said Brenda.

'What does our she look like?' asked Doreen.

'Like us only bigger, stupid,' said Susan. 'A giant tadpole.'

'How beautiful,' said Doreen, all dreamy eyed. 'A huge vision of smooth black loveliness.'

'Yes, yes,' said Brenda impatiently. 'Has anyone seen her?'

'No,' said everyone.

They had seen horrid wriggling things with sharp

pincers that had chased them out of the shadows. They had seen shiny black beetles swimming through the tiny seas carrying bubbles of air under their wings. They had seen dragonflies creeping down into the water to lay their eggs, and they had seen a giant green toad all covered in bumps and warts lumbering through the bulrushes. In every place there was life, some so small it could not be seen, but nowhere was there a sign of the giant tadpole that would be their mother.

'Apart from us everything else in this pond is ugly,' said Doreen.

'Especially the toad,' said Susan.

'Yuk,' said Brenda. 'I don't even want to talk about that disgusting thing, all green and warty.'

'Yeah,' said Susan, 'horrid gherkin face.'

The summer moved slowly on. The giant flowers on the waterlilies opened wide and turned their hearts towards the sun. The bulrushes grew taller and taller, casting their shadows longer and longer across the pond and out onto the grass. All day long the air was filled with a haze of flies. Swallows dived down between the trees catching the flies and dipping their heads in the smooth water. The garden grew fat and lazy. Animals dozed in the midsummer heat of July and those that did move did so with slow deliberation and only in the cool of evening. Under the midday sky, flowers drooped and trickled their pollen into the soft air. It seemed as if everything had slowed down to a complete standstill and the world would stay this way forever.

In the pond life slowed down too. For weeks the sun had shone down into the clear water until it was as tender as a warm bath. Even the darkest shadows under the lilies were warm, and great clouds of tiny water-fleas swam everywhere. The moorhens' eggs had hatched and as soon as their chicks had been old enough their parents had taken them back to the canal.

In the forest of slime things were happening to the tadpoles. Their soft black coats of velvet had changed to speckled brown and green and strange things were happening inside them.

'I don't half feel weird,' said Susan.

'How do you mean?' said Brenda.

'Well, sort of lumpy,' said Susan.

'Do you keep thinking about climbing out of the water?' said Doreen.

'Yes, I do. Do you?' said Susan.

'Yes,' said Doreen.

'Maybe we're not well,' said Brenda.

'Of course,' said Susan. 'That's it. That's why we're all off-colour.'

'I think we've got mumps,' said Doreen. 'That's why we all feel lumpy.'

'It's more than lumps,' said Brenda wriggling out from the leaf she'd been hiding behind. 'It's legs.'

The other tadpoles looked at her and sure enough she had two tiny legs growing out of her. She had shrunk too. Where there had been a long elegant tail Brenda now had a dumpy stump.

'Oh, that's awful,' said Susan backing away from Brenda. The others did the same and when Brenda stopped nibbling slime and ate a water-flea they all swam off feeling quite sick. But one by one they grew legs and not just two but four, and one by one their tails slowly disappeared and the strangest thing of all was that they all thought they looked rather good.

'My back legs are so big that I can jump right out of the water,' said Doreen.

'My back legs are so big that I can jump right over a mouse,' said Susan.

'Jumping's not so special,' said Brenda. 'Anyone can do that.'

'Oh yes?' said Susan. 'And what amazingly special thing have you got then?'

'Warts,' said Brenda. 'Great big wrinkly green warts.'

'So've I,' said Doreen. 'So've I.'

'We all have,' said Susan. 'We're all as warty as toads.'

There was a long silence. The tadpoles stood in the mud staring at their feet. They looked at each other and realised that they weren't tadpoles any more. They looked at the peaceful green toad all covered in bumps and warts lumbering through the bulrushes, the quiet brown-eyed giant they had called gherkin face, and realised that she was the mother they had all been looking for.

'You know,' said Brenda later that day when they had all crawled under a big wet stone. 'When you look at her closely, she really is incredibly beautiful.'

Geoff the Snail

'Come on, hurry up,' said Geoff the snail. 'If we don't get there soon, someone else will get it.'

'If we don't get there soon,' said his brother John, 'it will have turned into a fossil.'

The two snails were inside a milk bottle where they had been hibernating since the autumn. Early that morning the spring sunshine had shone through the glass until the damp air inside the bottle was as warm as a summer's day. The warmth had woken the two snails from their long sleep and in the grass outside they could see an old brown apple core. This was what they were now trying to reach.

'I'm starving,' said Geoff. 'In fact, I'm so hungry that I can't even remember when I last ate something.'

'That doesn't mean anything,' said John. 'Snails haven't got any memories. If something happened a few minutes ago us snails can't remember it.'

'Remember what?' said Geoff.

'Eh?'

'If I don't get something to eat soon,' said Geoff, 'my shell will fall off and I'll look like a slug.'

'Don't be disgusting,' said John. 'Horrible naked creatures.'

'Where?'

This is one of the reasons that snails are so slow. It isn't just that they move very slowly, but it's also that they keep forgetting why they are moving or where they are moving to.

'It's nice in here, isn't it?' said Geoff.

'Where?' said John.

'Hey, look out there,' said Geoff. 'An apple core.'

By the time John had turned round to look Geoff had forgotten what it was he was looking at.

'I think I'll go inside my shell for a bit,' he said, and disappeared.

'Who said that?' said John. When he couldn't

see anyone he got frightened and went back inside his shell too.

A bit later Geoff stuck his head out and said, 'I'm starving. In fact, I'm so hungry that I can't even remember when I last ate something.'

'That doesn't mean anything,' said John, reappearing too. 'Snails haven't got any memories. If something happened a few minutes ago us snails can't remember it.'

By the time they got outside it was raining and the apple core had started growing into a tree.

Joan the Sparrow

It was raining everywhere. It was the end of July and the air was warm and heavy. The heat of summer was caught and hemmed in by the rain that came down in heavy sheets. In sheltered places, under leaves and inside the old car, swarms of busy flies sheltered from the storm. Imprisoned by the rain they hovered in crowded confusion as they waited for it to pass.

The ancient car had stood at the bottom of the garden for thirty years. Its tyres were dull and cracked like the skin of an old rhinoceros and its wheels sunk deep into the ground. Tall grass and weeds grew everywhere hiding the dark spaces beneath the floor and creeping up inside the engine. For as long as anyone could remember there had been birds' nests inside it, and in the horse-hair seats there were families of mice. Spiders had laid cobwebs across the steering wheel and in the soft ferns growing on the damp floor was a world of silverfish and centipedes, a small jungle hidden away in a city garden.

Joan the sparrow stood on the back of one of the car seats and picked flies out of the air. There were so many she hardly had to lift a wing to catch them. In the glove compartment of the old car her five chicks were so fat they were almost falling out of the nest. Their adult feathers were nearly grown and in another few days they would be gone.

Summer had come so early that there would be time for a third brood. Joan had never had three lots of children in one summer before. She had met other sparrows who had, and in fact she had been the child of a third brood herself. The winter had come suddenly that year and her brothers and sisters hadn't survived the cold frosts. Joan had escaped by crawling into the heating vent of a café where she had stayed for three months, living on the fat that had collected on the pipes over the past twenty years. The sun had come out at Christmas and Joan had climbed out of her hideout to find the rest of her family gone.

The rain moved away and Joan flew out of the car into the warm sunshine. Everything was so rich and green that it was almost growing before her eyes. Joan's partner Charlie flew out from the bushes where he had been sheltering and they hopped across the lawn collecting the flies that hadn't survived the storm.

'The children will be off in a couple of days,' said Joan.

'Thank goodness for that,' said Charlie. 'We'll get a bit of peace at last.'

'Well, I had thought we could have a third brood,' said Joan. 'It's only July.'

'Oh, come on,' said Charlie. 'We're just about to get a bit of peace and quiet and you want to start all over again.'

'I know,' said Joan, 'but . . .'

'It'll be autumn soon,' Charlie added. 'It's time we were fattening ourselves up, never mind another lot of babies.'

'I know, I know.'

But it didn't matter what either of them said,

instinct held them in its grasp. They both knew the risks and they knew there wouldn't be a spare moment for the rest of the summer. While all the other animals in the garden were building up their strength for the winter, they would be using all theirs raising a new family that would probably be too young to survive the snow. They knew all these things but it made no difference. They had no choice. Because they could have children they would have children. That's how nature works. It never leaves any empty spaces. If it did, everything would have died out thousands of years ago.

So a few days later the second lot of chicks flew off into the garden and Charlie cleared out the nest in the old car. When it was ready Joan laid five more eggs. The days passed and she sat contentedly in the nest. Looking out of the little hole in the side of it she could see the back of the car seat. For fifteen years, since the door had fallen off, the wind and rain had blown into the old car and the seat that had once been bright red leather was now dull brown. There was grass growing in the folds where the leather had split and the mice that had lived inside the seat for generations were thinking of looking for somewhere warmer to live.

Joan watched for three days while a spider wove a beautiful web between the seat and the glove compartment. Backwards and forwards over and over again the spider went until she had finished. Then she came to a spot just below Joan's nest and waited for the flies to get caught in her trap. But she didn't get any flies, instead she caught a big fat sparrow called Charlie who swore and cursed as he pulled the cobwebs off his legs. And she also got eaten.

'I'll sit on the eggs for a bit, if you like,' said Charlie, hopping onto the nest.

'Yes, I could do with stretching my wings,' said Joan.

'There's a huge ants' nest down by the pond,' said Charlie, 'and there's loads of slugs on the cabbages.'

Inside their shells the tiny sparrows began to grow. The warm weather went on and on. It looked as if the third brood was going to be a success but then the man decided to move the car.

'Aunty Ferguson used to go to school in that car,' he said to his children. 'We'll take it into the garage and do it up.'

'But it's all rusted away,' said the boy.

'And the door's fallen off,' said the girl.

'And there's a garden growing inside it,' said the woman.

'We can fix all that,' said the man. 'When we've finished, it'll look like new.'

So they chopped down the weeds and bushes that had grown up round the car and propped it up on blocks of wood while they fitted new tyres and poured oil on the wheels. The children searched through the grass and found all the bits that had fallen off and carried them up to the house. Inside her nest Joan sat as still as midsummer's night while Charlie flew from branch to branch round the apple trees complaining loudly, but everyone was too busy with the car to notice him.

When the wheels were fixed they lowered the car to the ground and inch by inch pushed it slowly across the vegetable garden towards the garage at the side of the house. They rolled the car right across the vegetable beds, digging up carrots and cabbages as they went, until they reached the back of the garage.

When the car had been taken down to the bottom of the garden all those years before, there had been a flat lawn next to the garage. Now there were tall trees growing there with no way through.

'Well, we're not cutting the trees down,' said the man. 'We'll have to make a hole in the back of the garage.'

They took out the window in the back wall and got hammers and chisels and knocked out enough bricks to get the old car into the garage. When it was safely inside, they put all the bricks and the window back again and only then did they notice the two sparrows.

Charlie had followed the car into the garage and while the man had been cementing the bricks into place, he had sat up in the roof. Only when the window had been put in did the bird panic and flutter against the glass, but when the boy opened the window Charlie didn't fly out. Instead he flew inside the front of the car and then the children saw Joan sitting on her nest.

They left the window open so Joan and Charlie could come and go as they wanted. When the eggs hatched they were back and forwards all day long fetching food for the new chicks. The man, who liked to take life easy, was happy for an excuse to leave the car alone for a while. The children thought it was wonderful that a family of birds was actually living in part of their house.

When autumn came and the air grew cool the family of sparrows stayed safe and warm in their new home. Each day the children brought them food so that when the cold snows came they didn't have to go outside at all. The next spring when life began again they flew out into the world fat and healthy and happy.

Inside the garage the man blew the dust off his spanners and set to work on the car. It took him six years to finish it and all that time the sparrows' nest stayed where it was and every summer Joan laid three lots of eggs in it.

'You always said you wanted to move,' said Charlie as they sat in an apple tree looking down at the yellow patch of grass where the car had been.

'So I did,' said Joan, 'so I did.'

Dennis the Owl

There were seven large oak trees in the back garden and three more in the front. They were the oldest living things in the street and towered over everything, each one like a small forest in whose branches and leaves birds and squirrels and other creatures lived their lives. The trees had been there two hundred years before there had been any houses, and the oldest house was over a hundred years old. In one of the great oaks there were owls. They had lived there since the trees had been big enough to give them homes.

Owls are proud and dignified birds, as majestic as oak trees themselves.

Silent and sleeping during the day, at night they glide like soft ghosts through the darkness hunting small creatures that hurry across open fields and quiet hedgerows. Other animals keep away from owls and treat them with respect.

The two children who had come to live at fourteen had built their tree house in one of the oaks and in another close by lived Dennis the owl. At least, when he could find the right tree, he lived there. Quite often he would come back at dawn and land on the wrong tree. He would swoop down through the wrong branches and smash the top of his head into the wrong trunk exactly in the place where the hole he lived in should have been.

'Someone's stolen my house again,' he would say as the stars spun round in his head. 'You go out to get your dinner, not wanting to bother anyone, and while you're out someone steals your house.'

If the weather was warm he would just stay where he was and if it was cold he would flutter unsteadily down to the old car and sleep on the back seat. Sometimes as he sat there it would start raining and he would wake up with water running down his neck and wonder what he was doing wrong.

'I'm sure life should be better than this,' he said to no one. 'All I want is a warm place to sleep and a nice soft mouse for supper. And people to stop hiding my house. And crunchy moths for breakfast and warm slugs for tea.'

'And a friend.'

'And a dry neck.'

The trouble was that Dennis wasn't a proud and dignified bird. He was lost and lonely and not very clever. Nature seemed to have only a certain amount of brains to give out and by the time Dennis had hatched, his three sisters had got them all and there was none left for him.

'Better to have a kind heart,' his mother used to say, ' than be as clever as . . .'

'As clever as an owl,' said his sisters, laughing and pointing at him.

'. . . and have nobody love you,' continued his mother.

He was all alone now. His mother had gone a long time ago and so had his sisters. On still summer nights he sometimes thought he could hear the hooting of another owl far away but he had never seen one.

'What use is a kind heart,' he said to himself, 'if no one knows you've got one?'

Most of the time it was all right, he just got on with things. His house was quite often in the right place. He found plenty of slugs and bits and pieces to eat and he didn't think about anything. Sometimes though, there were dark days when the sun refused to shine in the sky or in his head. On those days he sat in the shadows of his home unable to move. Sadness wrapped him up in its arms and filled him with a terrible loneliness.

'All I want . . .' he said to himself, but he didn't know what it was.

'All I want is something.'

The mood would pass and the next night he would be out at dusk with a huge appetite searching up and down the towpath for mice. In his whole life he had never caught a mouse. The mice had soon realised that Dennis was not like other owls. They realised that they were much cleverer than he was and, although they could never hope to be able to run fast enough if he swooped down on them, they could still stop him eating them.

One would keep watch and as soon as Dennis

approached he would shout, 'TSP ALERT,' at the top of his voice. The mice called him TSP which stood for Two Short Planks.

'Because that's what he's as thick as,' they said.

As Dennis swooped, the mice rolled onto their backs, tucked up their legs and sang:

'We are just potatoes.
Cut us into strips,
Fry us in a pan
And make us into chips.'

'You look like mice to me,' said Dennis.

'No, no,' sang the mice:

'We really are potatoes.
Boil us in a pan,
Mash us up with butter
And eat us with some ham.'

'Potatoes can't speak,' said Dennis, feeling a bit unsure of himself.

'For goodness sake,' sang the mice:

'Listen stupid owl.
You wearing earplugs?
We're all just round potatoes.
Fly off and eat some slugs.'

And that was what poor Dennis did. Every night he shuffled around under the bushes scraping up the grass like an old chicken and eating slugs and beetles. It was no life for an owl. His feathers were broken and muddy, his claws were worn down and his back ached from all the bending over. There were thousands of slugs but no matter how many he ate part of him always felt empty. As the sun began to rise he went back home to bed and wondered if it would be like this forever.

His sleep was full of dreams of when he had been young, of the long summer after his sisters had gone and he had had his mother all to himself. The days were full of sunshine pouring into the warm nest inside the tree. He sunk into the soft feathers and moss and slept until evening. When it was dark his mother flew in and fed him with soft strips of meat and sweet moths. Like the best summers of childhood it had seemed to go on forever and ever.

Now it was all just a fuzzy memory.

When the people had arrived it had hardly effected Dennis. The crows had come to live in the trees after they had been pushed out of the chimneys and it had become a lot noiser. The children had built a wooden house in the next tree, but none of it had made much difference to the lonely owl. By the time he came out at night, the children were back indoors and the crows were fast asleep. The rest of the animals in the garden generally ignored him. Most of them were asleep too and the other night creatures were too busy making their own livings to be bothered with a miserable owl.

He had tried talking to other animals, but they didn't want to know. He tried hanging round outside the rabbit warren at the bottom of the garden but the rabbits just thought he was trying to eat their babies and slipped out of the back door. He tried talking to the hedgehogs but they were making so much noise crashing through the grass and sucking snails out of their shells that they didn't hear him. He even tried talking to the sparrow that was nesting in the old car but she sank down into the darkness and pretended she wasn't there.

'All I want is a friend,' said Dennis. 'It doesn't even have to be a special friend, just someone who will talk to me.'

'I'd just like to be a little bit important to someone,' he said to no one.

There were wild cats across the canal in the derelict factories but when Dennis went near them they hissed and spat at him and cut the air with their claws. An ordinary owl who caught mice and screeched at the moon wouldn't have been scared of cats but Dennis was a gentle soul and even the kittens chased him away. The foxes that lived along the canal pretended he wasn't there.

In his whole life only one animal, apart from his mother, had been kind to him, and that had been an old horse. One moonlit night a barge had tied up at the bottom of the garden. The giant horse that pulled it stood silently under the overhanging branches of the oak trees. The round windows of the boat glowed yellow like a row of pale suns and thin smoke trickled up into the cloudless sky making a pale ribbon across the moon. Dennis flew down to the fence by the towpath. He had never seen a horse before.

'Hello,' he said.

'Hello,' said the horse.

'You're not a potato, are you?' said Dennis. The horse took a few steps backwards.

'Er, no,' said the horse. And realising Dennis was a bit strange he added, 'You're not are you?'

'No,' said Dennis. 'I'm an owl.'

'Yes,' said the horse, 'I thought you were.'

'Well, you were right,' said Dennis. In the bushes behind him there was a crashing sound as three young rabbits fell laughing off the pile of twigs they had climbed up. The horse leant down and took a mouthful of grass. Dennis sat on the fence and watched him. An hour later the horse was still eating grass and Dennis was still watching him.

'Did you want something?' asked the horse.

'Well, I was wondering,' said Dennis, 'if you'd be my friend.'

'Mmm,' said the horse, 'I'm actually a bit busy at the moment.'

'Well, when you're not busy,' said Dennis. 'How about then?'

'All right then,' said the horse. 'Come back tomorrow.' But tomorrow never came, for the next night the barge and the horse were twenty miles away and Dennis never saw them again.

And then his whole life changed.

One night the man was driving home down country lanes. The rain threw itself out of the sky in a violent summer thunderstorm and as the car went round a bend the man saw something flapping in the middle of the road. He stopped and in the headlights' beam he saw a bird with a broken wing. It was struggling towards the side of the road, dragging its wing through the crashing rain.

The man got out of the car and wrapped the bird up in his coat. It was a wild-eyed owl and although he was rescuing it, it tried to attack the man as he carried it back to his car. He laid it on the back seat and went home.

For the next few weeks the injured owl lived in the garage. It hid away in the darkness up in the beams of the roof staring down at its rescuers with wild yellow eyes. The vet came and mended its wing but it was never able to fly again. It looked down at the food the children brought but only when they had gone and it was quiet again would it flutter down to eat. Even after a month when all its bones were mended and the feathers it had lost were growing back again, it wouldn't let any of the family go near it.

'She can live in the garden,' said the man. 'And we'll have to feed her for the rest of her life.'

'She can live in our tree house,' said the boy and that's what she did. They filled in the sides that faced into the wind and made a perch from a broom handle. And when everything was ready and she had her bandages removed, the man put on a pair of thick gloves and carried her up the ladder to her new home. They tethered her to the perch to stop her falling out of the tree until she got used to it and went back into the house.

'Maybe she'll get better one day,' said the boy, 'and fly away.'

'I think we'll call her Audrey,' said the girl.

Audrey sat on her perch looking out into the twilight. It was the middle of June and below her in an apple tree a blackbird was singing its summer song. The bats were up and about, swooping in and out of the trees chasing flies.

I wonder what they taste like, thought Audrey. *Bats that is, not flies.*

They flew so fast that she had never caught one and she certainly wasn't going to now.

If she stretched her legs and leant right forward, she could see right down to the ground below. A hedgehog was drinking at the edge of a little pond. Audrey had to drink out of a tin cup.

If the man hadn't picked me up, she thought, *I wouldn't be drinking out of a tin cup.*

She thought back to the night of the storm. She had been hunting far away from home when it had started and in her rush to get back she had flown straight into a telephone wire and broken her wing. She thought of her home in the sycamore tree in the middle of a large wood, and as she sat there daydreaming she almost missed the black shape flying right in front of her. It was silhouetted across the evening sky, a shape just like her own.

'Hey,' she shouted and the shape crashed into a tree.

'Ow,' said a voice in the darkness.

'Over here,' she called.

'Where?'

This went on for a while, but at last Dennis stood on the edge of the tree house looking at Audrey.

'You're an owl,' he said.

'Well, I'm not a potato,' said Audrey.

'I can see that,' said Dennis. 'You haven't got any fur or paws.'

'What?' said Audrey.

'Well . . .' Dennis started to explain.

'It's all right,' said Audrey, 'don't tell me.'

'Will you be my friend?' said Dennis.

Audrey looked over the edge of the tree house and said, 'See those little furry things running round down there.'

'Yes,' said Dennis, 'the potatoes.'

'Er, yes,' said Audrey, 'the potatoes. Well, if you go and get me one of those, I'll be your friend.'

'All right.'

Dennis flew down and although the mice rolled up as small as they could and sang every song they knew, it did no good. Dennis had a friend and his friend liked potatoes.

A week later the man took the tether off Audrey's leg and, although she never flew properly again, she hopped and fluttered from branch to branch through the great oak trees. And in the spring she fluttered into Dennis's nest and laid four eggs and a month later he had four more friends and was so busy catching potatoes that he never had time to be lonely again.

Metamorphosis

Beneath green leaves,
In hard cocoons,
In tunnels damp and cold,
Nature's heat turns night to day
Rebuilds the tired and old.

She holds the thing
So small and drab
In the focus of her eye,
Takes ashes from a fading fire
And builds a butterfly.

The Five Dorises

DorisEthel the chicken was teaching her five chicks how to catch worms. She had taken them to a newly dug bed of earth in the vegetable garden where she scratched about with her feet and then jumped back, head to one side, to see what she had uncovered. The chicks were bored. They had all the food they wanted brought to them by the children and they couldn't see the point of grubbing about in a load of mud. They had scraped up a row of radishes and wanted to do something else.

'Mum,' said Doris One, 'can we go and play?'

'Yeah, Mum,' said Doris Four, 'we're fed up.'

'Listen children,' said DorisEthel. 'This is very important. It's the most important thing you will ever learn.'

'What, rummaging about in the earth for those horrible worm things?' said Doris Two.

'Yes,' said DorisEthel. 'It's what chickens do. All over the world there are chickens scraping up the dirt and eating worms and slugs.'

'Well, I'm not going to,' said Doris Three. 'I'm going to eat porridge.'

'Me too,' said Doris Five.

'And us,' said the other three Dorises.

'And cake,' said Doris Three. 'Don't forget the cake we got last Sunday.'

DorisEthel could see that she was wasting her time. The chicks were in an awkward mood and no amount of talking would make them change their mind. Maybe she was old-fashioned but she could think of nothing more wonderful than pulling a big wet worm out of the soft earth and feeling it wriggle down her throat as she swallowed it.

'Children today,' she sighed, and waddled off across the lawn towards the house.

'Cake indeed,' she said. 'What's the world

coming to? When I was their age we had to eat second-hand caterpillars and newspapers.'

Mind you, she thought to herself, *it was nice cake, especially the raisins all slimy in the middle like slugs.*

'What are we going to do now?' said Doris One as the chicks rushed after the old hen.

'Play,' said Doris Two.

'Go on then,' said Doris Four, 'do it.'

'Do what?' said Doris Two.

'Play.'

'Er, right then,' said Doris Two, 'come on.' She scuttled up the back doorstep and wriggled through the cat flap into the house. The four other chicks ran after her, landing one after the other on the mat. DorisEthel tried to get through the flap after her children but she was too fat. She paced up and down outside the door clucking loudly and calling them. Inside, the five chicks pretended they couldn't hear her. They stood in the middle of the kitchen floor and looked around.

'Is this playing, then?' said Doris Three.

'Yes,' said Doris Two.

'It's great, isn't it?' said Doris Five.

'What are we going to do now?' said Doris One.

'We could eat the cat food,' said Doris Three.

'Cat food?' said Doris Four nervously. 'Do you mean there's a cat in here?'

'Well, if there's a cat flap, there must be a cat,' said Doris Three.

'What, a big cat with teeth and claws and stuff?' said Doris Four.

'Errr, yes,' said Doris Three, looking round.

'I want my mummy,' cried Doris Four, running back to the door. The other chicks rushed after her and they all collided in a great heap on the mat.

'Mum, Mum,' Doris Four cried as they scrambled out into the garden, 'there's a giant cat after us.'

'It's going to eat us all up,' said Doris Three. The five chicks ran as fast they could across the lawn and back into the hen house. DorisEthel, who knew there wasn't a cat in the house, waddled slowly after them. Inside the hut all the chicks jumped into the nesting box and hid in the straw, except Doris Four who jumped on top of the box and pretended to be brave.

'Cock-a-doodle,' she shouted.

'Who said that?' said DorisEthel as she came into the hut.

'It wasn't me,' said Doris Three.

'It wasn't us,' said Doris One and Doris Five.

'Said what?' said Doris Two.

'That cock-a-doodle noise,' said DorisEthel.

'Sorry, Mum,' said Doris Four. 'It just sort of came over me.'

'Do you know what it means?' said DorisEthel.

'No. I don't even know why I said it,' said Doris Four.

'Is it rude?' said Doris Three. The four chicks in the nest box started sniggering and nudging each other.

'It's rude. It's rude,' they chorused.

'No it isn't,' said DorisEthel. 'It means that Doris Four is a boy.'

The four chicks in the nest box giggled even more.

'No I'm not,' said Doris Four. 'I'm a chicken.'

'Yes, of course you are,' said DorisEthel, 'but you're a boy chicken. You're a cockerel.'

The other four Dorises jumped out of the nest box and stared up at Doris Four. He looked very confused and shuffled off to the back where they couldn't see him. But a cockerel he was and there was no getting away from it.

'I don't want to be a boy,' he said. 'I won't say it any more.' But he couldn't stop himself. He felt the words coming up inside him and he clenched his little beak shut as tight as he could but he just couldn't stop them.

'COCK-A-DOODLE-DOO!' he shouted at the top of his tiny voice.

'Wow,' said Doris Three. 'That was great.'

Her sisters thought it was great too, but no one thought it was as great as DorisEthel did. She fluffed her feathers out with pride. Over the summer Doris Four grew into a magnificent cockerel and once again the days began with a great crowing as he stood proud and tall on the shed roof and woke the sleeping world. And once again, like Eric before him, he got soaked to the skin as next door's upstairs window opened and a bucketful of water came flying out.

Doris Four's sisters had grown up too and were laying eggs every day. The hen house was a constant bustle with clucking and crowing and the children forever in and out. It was all too much for DorisEthel so she went back to the peace and quiet of her apple box to dream of days gone by when she too had been part of it all.

'If he's a cockerel,' said the boy, 'we can't call him Doris any more.'

'We'll call him Kevin,' said the little girl.

'No, no,' said the boy. 'We'll call him Boris.'

And that's what they did, though to his sisters and DorisEthel he was always known as DorisBoris.

Arnold the Mouse

As night fell over the quiet streets the animals that slept through the day began to wake up. In dark tunnels and soft nests, creatures stirred and opened their eyes. They stretched their legs and wings, tasted the evening air and thought of breakfast.

For a few it would be the last night of their lives. Hedgehogs, blinded by two suns, would be squashed by cars. Mice, racing across open lawns, would be food for cats and owls. But for most of the animals, living by night was safer than living by day. In the darkness they could slip into places unseen and while the rest of the world slept they could live their lives in peace.

As the sky disappeared, the rabbits came out of their burrows. With eyes still full of sleep they sniffed the fresh air and spread out across the garden and canal bank. They crept into next door's garden and ate their way along the neat rows of flowers. The nervous man and his thin wife put wire netting along the fence but the rabbits just went underneath it. On warm summer evenings next door's cat sat on the patio and watched them. The moles burrowed under the lawn and threw up piles of earth on to the neatly clipped grass, and on calm nights spiders spun their webs between tall grass and low branches.

This night was a calm night. It was so quiet that Arnold the mouse could hear the traps going off in the other houses along the street. He rolled over in his nest of newspaper under the kitchen floor and a shiver ran down his back as he thought of his fellow mice coming to such a violent end.

There were no traps in his house; at least, not the steel spring type that killed you. In his house the trap was a warm and welcoming plastic box and inside it was a piece of fabulous cheese. Every night Arnold crept into the trap and ate the cheese. And every night he tripped over the bar and the door fell shut behind him. Twenty-two times he had done it and twenty-two times at eight o'clock in the morning the man had carried the trap down to the bottom of the garden and tipped Arnold out through a gap in the hedge onto the canal bank. It was the same every day. Arnold knew the routine so well that if he ran as fast as possible he could be back in the house before the man was.

On the twenty-third day the man said, 'I'm sure that's the same mouse we caught yesterday.'

Brilliant, thought Arnold. *I'm sharing my home with an idiot.*

The children peered through the brown plastic at Arnold and said. 'How can you tell?'

Great, thought Arnold. *They're all idiots.*

'Isn't it incredible?' he said to his wife, Edna, when he was back under the kitchen floor for the twenty-fourth time. 'I can understand how maybe they can't tell each other apart. I mean, all humans look the same, but how on earth they can't see it's me every time is beyond me.'

'They're idiots,' said Edna.

'That's what I reckon,' said Arnold.

The twenty-fifth time, the man tipped Arnold

out into his hand and tried to paint a red spot on his fur. Arnold bit the man on the thumb and the man dropped him on the floor. Arnold ran under the kitchen units and back into his nest. The twenty-sixth time, the man put a big thick pair of gloves on and Arnold ended up with a red blob on his head. The next night, just to confuse the man, Edna went in the trap.

'Arnie, you're wicked, you are,' she said to Arnold when she came back from the bottom of the garden the next morning, 'taking advantage of simple people like that.'

Arnold thought of bringing all his friends and relations in and getting them to go into the trap one by one, but he didn't like the idea of giving up his nightly meal of cheese and the next night he went back in the trap.

'Look,' cried the man, 'it is the same mouse.'

'The bottom of the garden's not far enough away,' said the woman. 'You'll have to take it right down the street.'

'But it might get run over,' said the man.

'Well, tip it out into someone's garden,' said the woman. 'It can go and bother them.'

182

The man went to the end of the short street and when no one was looking tipped Arnold over the hedge into the last garden. Arnold had been there many times before. In fact, he had relatives who lived there. So, he dusted himself off and ran along behind the fences following the man back home.

'I hope this isn't going to become a habit,' he said when he was back in the kitchen again.

'It's the cheese that's a habit,' said Edna. 'If you stopped going after the cheese you wouldn't keep getting caught.'

'I like cheese,' said Arnold.

'Like cheese!' said Edna. 'It's a bit more than like, isn't it? You're a cheeseaholic.'

'No I'm not,' said Arnold. 'I'm just very fond of a bit of cheese.'

'All right then,' said Edna. 'Let's see. When he puts the trap down tonight, don't go in it.'

'All right, then.'

'I bet you can't do it,' said Edna. 'I bet you can't stay out of the trap all night.'

'Of course I can, it's easy,' said Arnold. 'What do you bet me?'

'Whatever you like,' said Edna.

'All right,' said Arnold. 'I bet you a piece of Wensleydale.'

'See,' said Edna. 'All you can think about is cheese.'

And she was right. Before he went to bed, the man put the trap in the kitchen cupboard. Inside it was a delicious, ripe, sweating piece of Stilton. Its powerful, thrilling perfume filled the whole room. Arnold buried his head in the nest but he could still smell it. He tried to sleep but it was impossible. At midnight he went out into the garden to find something else to eat and to get away from the beautiful temptation, but it was useless. He couldn't get it out of his mind.

He went for a run along the towpath. He ran and ran until the house was miles behind him and his lungs were thumping like a tiny steam engine. But no matter what he did it was no good. Every time he blinked he could see the open door of the trap in his mind and glowing in its heart like a piece of the moon was the pale, irresistible cheese. The new day was hiding just below the horizon and Arnold knew that if he didn't get home before it was light, something with sharp claws would have him for breakfast.

'I could stay here,' he said to himself. 'Hide in a dark hole until tomorrow night and then go home.' But he knew he wouldn't. He knew he would go home and he knew he would go into the trap and eat the cheese. Edna was right, and he'd known it all along.

So, as the sun crept up into the sky and the early birds flew down to catch the worms, Arnold crawled wearily back through the fence at the bottom of the garden, crossed the lawn and slipped into the house. Edna was sitting by the trap waiting for him.

'I tried,' he said. 'I really did.'

'I know, I saw you,' said Edna as Arnold walked into the trap and the door dropped shut behind him.

'It's come back,' said the man. 'That wretched mouse has come back again.'

'You'll have to take it somewhere in the car,' said the woman. 'Drive out into the country and stick it under a bush.'

'Do you think it will be all right?' said the man.

'Of course it will,' said the woman. 'There are hundreds of mice in the country. It'll go and live with them.'

She didn't know that the other mice wouldn't

accept Arnold, that every time he tried to go into their homes they would drive him out. So the man put the trap on the back seat of the car and set off for the country.

They drove for miles and miles until they left the last house behind and were surrounded by moonlit fields. In a quiet lane by some trees the man knelt down in the grass and opened the trap. Arnold looked out and refused to leave. The man pulled the back off the trap and pushed Arnold out with his finger. Then he got back in the car and drove away.

Arnold ran deep into the grass until he found a small dark place to hide. All day he lay there curled up into a small pathetic ball. In his heart he felt a hopeless loneliness and in his mind a lifeless nothing. He knew he had lost Edna and the perfect garden forever. He had grown up there and so had his parents before him and now it was all gone because of his weakness.

I wish I was dead, he thought. *I am such a pathetic creature.*

When night fell he walked out into the moonlight into a wide open space and waited for an owl to swoop down and end his miserable life. But no owl came and by three o'clock in the morning Arnold was stiff and hungry.

Maybe if I sit here long enough, he thought, *I'll catch a cold and die.*

By five o'clock it was light and suddenly Arnold felt frightened and ran back to the safety of the dark hole. As he ran in, he tripped over a hazelnut that had fallen from the tree above. When an owl hadn't got him and it had been too warm to catch cold, he had thought of starving himself to death. But he hadn't eaten for nearly twenty-four hours and had such a tummyache that he sat down and ate the hazelnut.

'I'm so pathetic,' he said to himself as he fell asleep, 'that I can't do anything right.' And in his dreams he was running down a hill with a giant round cheese rolling after him. Just as he reached the safety of a gate he tripped and fell and the cheese rolled right over him and covered him from head to tail in red wax.

Back at the house Edna was more angry than sad. Her stupid Arnold had lost everything through no one's fault but his own. She had done her best to keep him out of the trap but nothing she had said had stopped him. He deserved everything that had happened to him.

'All the same,' she said to her sister Janet, 'I do miss him.'

'You're better off without him,' said Janet.

'You're probably right,' said Edna. 'But I miss him something awful.'

'You'll find someone else. Just wait and see,' said Janet. She was losing patience with Edna and went off into the garden to catch slugs.

'I don't want anyone else,' said Edna, 'I just want my Arnie.'

Then she had an idea. It wasn't a great idea but it was the only one she had and besides, she had nothing to lose. All her children had grown up and gone away. She had nothing to stay in the kitchen for, so she might as well try it.

'If I keep going into the trap,' she said to Janet, 'maybe they'll take me to the same place they took Arnie.'

'That's a ridiculous idea,' said Janet, but Edna had made her mind up and every night for the next week she went and ate the cheese and got caught. The humans weren't very bright. They didn't take her to the country straight away. After six days they painted a red spot on her back and on the seventh day the man took her to the end of the street.

'It isn't going to work,' said Janet. 'You're just wasting your time.' But she wasn't, because on the eighth day the man and the woman got in the car and drove her out into the country. They stopped the car, opened the trap and Edna ran off deep into the grass until she found a small dark place to hide.

It was warm in the dark place and the air was filled with the smell of damp fur and hazelnuts. Something was snoring at the back of the hole and Edna tip-toed nervously into the darkness. Towards the back it was so dark she couldn't see. She walked blindly forward, tripped over a broken nut shell and went flying. She landed on something soft and hairy that wriggled and swore at her.

'Arnie?' she said. 'Is that you?'

'Edna?' said the soft hairy thing. 'Is that you?'

And of course it was. It was both of them and, although they never went back to the perfect garden, and although there were no more meals of Stilton, they both lived happily ever after.

A year later people came and had a picnic under

the hazel tree and when they had gone there was a cheese sandwich left behind. Old dreams came back into Arnold's head, dreams that had gone to sleep. He nibbled away the bread and there it was, a thick slice of cheddar; but when he tasted it, the magic had faded.

'I wonder what I ever saw in it,' he said, and later that night a passing fox picked up the sandwich and took it away.

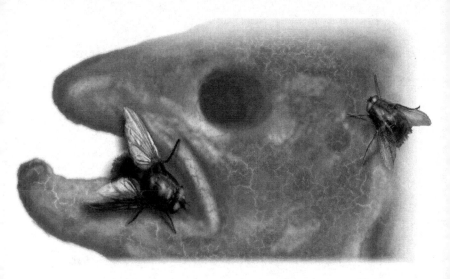

Attila the Bluebottle

There are times when life is perfect. For Attila the bluebottle it was one of those times. When he actually thought about it, every single day of his life had been perfect and he had been alive for a whole week.

He had spent the morning inside a fish head at the bottom of the dustbin and was so full up he could hardly move. Everywhere he looked it was the same view of paradise. Fat lazy bluebottles full of rotten fish staggered around with big contented grins on their faces.

'I'm so full,' said Attila, 'that if you gave me a rat covered in slime I wouldn't be able to eat a mouthful.'

'I'm so full,' said his sister Lucille, 'that if the rat covered in slime had been lying at the bottom of a sewer for a year, I wouldn't be able to eat half a mouthful.'

'I'm so full . . . ' said Attila.

'Okay,' said their mother, 'we get the picture.'

'Here,' said Attila, 'do you want to hear a joke.'

'Yeah, go on then,' said Lucille.

'This isn't the Only Joke, is it?' said their mother.

'No, no,' said Attila, 'I just made it up.'

'Go on then,' said their mother.

'Right. Two flies are standing on a dead dog . . .'

'That's brilliant,' said Lucille.

'That's not it,' said Attila. 'I haven't finished.'

'It is the Only Joke,' said his mother. 'I know it is.'

'Go on, go on,' said Lucille.

'Two flies are standing on a dead dog and one says to the other, "Is that your dead dog?"'

'Yeah, go on,' said Lucille, hopping about on all her feet.

'And the other fly says . . .'

'. . . No, just carrion,' said their mother with a sigh.

'Oh Mum,' said Attila.

'I don't get it,' said Lucille.

While Attila explained the joke to Lucille, their mother beat her head against the rotten fish until she was sick.

'Hey Mum, that's brilliant,' said Attila. 'Can you show us how to do that?'

'Oh, go and stick your head in a disinfectant bottle,' said his mother and went off to the other side of the dustbin. When she got there she wriggled though the rubbish until she found a green pork chop. Then she laid six hundred eggs.

'What's the matter with her?' asked Lucille.

'Dunno,' said Attila. 'Maybe she's got no sense of humour.'

Someone lifted the lid and emptied a bucket of slops into the dustbin. The falling rubbish flattened some of the flies and sent dozens of others buzzing up into the air. Attila and Lucille had been skiing inside the fish head and when the lid had been put back on they crawled out to inspect the latest delivery.

'Yuk,' said Lucille, 'it's all bits of vegetables and fruit peelings.'

'Isn't there any meat at all?' asked Attila.

'Can't see any.'

'What about fish?'

'No.'

'Cheese rind?'

'No,' said Lucille, 'nor jam. It's all just tea bags and cabbage leaves.'

'You know what this means, don't you?' said Attila.

'No.'

'It means they've turned vegetarian,' said Attila. 'It's the end of civilisation as we know it.'

'What are we going to do?' said Lucille.

'We'll have to go somewhere else, I suppose.'

'What do you mean?' said Lucille.

'You know,' said Attila, 'move.'

'What, like Mum,' said Lucille, 'over behind the dirty nappy mountain?'

'No, no,' said Attila, 'right away.'

'What, as far as the lake of slime, right at the bottom of the dustbin?' said Lucille.

'Further than that,' said Attila. 'Right out of the dustbin, into Nowhere.'

'You're mad, you are,' said Lucille. 'We can't live out there.'

'Yes we can. Where do you think we came from in the first place?'

'The Big Fish,' said Lucille. 'We came from inside The Big Fish.'

'No, no,' said Attila, 'where did flies come from before that?'

'I don't understand,' said Lucille.

Attila couldn't think of the right words to say. He wasn't even sure there were any right words; but the one thing he was sure of was that if they didn't leave, they would starve. Lucille understood this and although she was terrified she waited with Attila under the rim and the next time the lid was lifted they flew out into Nowhere.

Inside the dustbin it had always been damp and cool. It had always been dark too, except when the sky lifted and more food fell in. Then there had been a flash of brilliant light like an exploding sun.

Now it was all brilliant light. At first Attila and Lucille were completely blinded. They flew frantically upwards expecting to hit something at any moment but there was nothing there. As their eyes became accustomed to the sunshine, they saw the roof of the house below them and flew down to the sea of grey slates and rested. Far below them a child had just put the dustbin lid back and was going into the house.

'Is this heaven then?' said Lucille nervously.

'I don't think so,' said Attila. 'I think you have to be dead to go to heaven and I don't think we are.'

Flies don't live long enough to sit and think about things too much. It's light, it's dark. It's hot, it's cold. This rat's leg tastes delicious. They never have to think about money or clean shoes. Life for flies is very simple. Attila and Lucille's mother had told them that the inside of the dustbin was the whole universe and they had believed her. After all, it was obvious, the inside of the dustbin was all they could see.

But now they were outside and they could see a lot more. They could see that their dustbin was just one small space in one small garden and that each house down the street had a dustbin of its own.

'So much for listening to Mum,' said Attila.

'Yeah,' said Lucille, 'what did she know. She was only two weeks older than us.'

'Two weeks is a long time,' said Attila. 'It's nearly a lifetime.'

'Yeah, I suppose so,' said Lucille. 'Let's have lunch.'

They flew across the garden in a great sweeping curve that they never could have done inside the dustbin. An old chicken was scratching about in the grass and round her feet five yellow chicks darted about like fluffy beetles. The chicken was picking up slugs and feeding them to her children, but as soon as she turned her back the children spat them out. The two bluebottles had never eaten slug before.

'It's quite nice,' said Attila, 'but not as good as fish heads.'

'They're probably too fresh,' said Lucille. 'If you kept them in rotten egg for a week or two they'd probably taste better.'

After lunch they went and sat on the kitchen window sill. The sun had made the stone warm and the two flies felt quite drowsy.

'Do you suppose everything Mum told us was untrue?' said Lucille.

'How do you mean?' asked Attila.

'You know. All that stuff about The Big Fish,' said Lucille.

'What, and the inside of the dustbin being the whole world?' said Attila.

'Yes.'

'Yes, I suppose it must have been,' said Attila. 'After all, when you think about it, it does all seem ridiculous.'

'You mean there's no Giant Flypaper and no Killer Aerosol?' said Lucille sarcastically.

'No, of course not,' said Attila. The two bluebottles laughed so much that all their eyes watered. Someone opened the window behind them and a thick sweet sugary smell drifted out. It rolled over them like a dream and made them feel quite giddy. They flew onto the window frame and looked into the kitchen. In the middle of the table was a thick warm lemon meringue pie fresh from the oven.

'Isn't that wonderful?' said Lucille. 'Let's go and get some.'

'Hang on, hang on,' said Attila. 'What do you think we are – wasps? We're bluebottles. We eat rotten meat and dead fish.'

'But it smells so good,' said Lucille. 'Couldn't we just go and lick it a bit?'

'No, of course we can't,' said Attila, 'but I tell you what we could do.'

'What, what?'

'We could go and be sick on it.'

So the two bluebottles flew into the house and buzzed round and round the kitchen table, their heads all dizzy with the luscious smell of hot sugar. And there in the hot summer kitchen they discovered that not everything their mother had told them had been wrong. They had learnt that the world was a huge and wonderful place full of light and wide open skies. They had learnt that everywhere there were new and amazing things, that there was so much to see and to do, it seemed as if an endless life of adventure stretched out before them. And the very last thing they learnt as they swooped down towards the soft meringue mountains was that their mother had certainly been right about one thing – The Massive Rolled Up Newspaper.

Arkwright the Cat

Winter came to the garden and plants that had stood tall and green all summer turned to gold and crumbled to dust. The skeletons of great thistles stood brown and lifeless, their dangerous spikes now no more than frail icicles crisp with frost. Between their shrivelled leaves the shells of insects turned to paper and blew away in the wind.

The swallows had gone to Africa leaving their nests to sleeping spiders while above them tortoiseshell butterflies hibernated in the roof. The birds that remained grew silent and lazy. They sat huddled in the bare branches fluffed up against the cold. With the flowers dead and gone the insects that had lived off them died too.

Below the old shed at the bottom of the garden the hedgehogs sank deep into their nest of grass and slept. The worms moved deeper into the earth to escape the cold and the moles tunnelled deeper to find them. At the bottom of the pond next year's mosquitos and dragonflies lay suspended in tiny eggs and above the city the timeless stars flickered in the clear cold air of night.

Nature slowed down until it had almost stopped.

In the yard beside the house the wind picked up the loose leaves and threw them in a pile by the back door until it had made a golden pyramid against the step. It whistled round the corner and rattled past the dustbins as sharp as a rusty knife. Arkwright the cat sat in the coal bunker and listened as the wind roared round the house.

Maybe it's just my memory playing tricks, he thought to himself, *but the wind seemed softer in the old days.*

Maybe it's because I'm getting old, he thought, *and my fur is growing thin, but it didn't seem to be so cold either.*

He drifted off into dreams of long hot summer days when he and Gertrude had been the most feared creatures along the whole canal. No bird or mouse had been safe as they swept like tigers through the grass. Even tiny moths had flown away as they approached.

The years had passed and they had grown old and slow. A year ago Gertrude had crept into a tunnel under a mountain of old railway sleepers. Arkwright had sat by the dark hole and waited but he had known she wasn't coming out again.

A sparrow hopped down the yard but Arkwright was too cold to move. All he had eaten for the past few days had been the last moths of autumn that had flown into the streetlights. There was nothing much else to eat in this quiet tidy street. It wasn't the sort of place where people threw scraps out. He'd found a few crusts thrown out for the birds but as soon as people saw him on their lawns they chased him away. He had grown so thin that every breath of cold reached into his bones.

He had grown up wild among the factories across the canal. There were dozens of cats there, dirty scraggy creatures that fought and screamed in the night.

He had had his day, when he had been top cat and all the others moved aside as he'd passed. It hadn't lasted long. It never did. After one proud summer when he was five years old another younger cat had pushed him aside and over the next five years he had moved further and further away from the centre of things until he found himself with the old cats who scratched around in the younger ones' leftovers. His companions then had been one-eared, half-blind, limping creatures hiding in dark corners. Arkwright hadn't been like the rest of them. He still had all his ears and teeth and, although slowed by age, he still walked straight and proud.

After Gertrude died Arkwright felt restless and unwelcome. He sat by the canal and looked across the brown water at the tall trees and thick bushes alive with birds and butterflies, and said to himself, *That's where I'll go, over there to that beautiful garden.*

He walked along the canal in both directions for miles and miles but there was no way across. From time to time an old barge moved slowly along the water with its engine purring softly like a heartbeat. The warm smells of coal fires and cooking food drifted across the water as they passed. Ducks moved lazily aside and then the canal fell quiet again. If he had been younger he would have jumped onto one and waited until it had gone close to the opposite bank and leapt off, but he was too tired and stiff in his bones. So he just sat and watched them as they went by.

'How can I get across the water?' he asked the other cats.

'Too good to live here with the rest of us, are you?' they said and stopped speaking to him. Arkwright left the old lorry where most of the cats lived and moved into an oil drum by the towpath. And then one winter night there was a great storm and lightning struck a giant oak and it fell across the canal crushing the lorry as it came. In the morning when the wind and rain had faded away there was a path over the water to the wonderful garden. The other cats had fled into the desert of factories, too scared to go near the wrecked lorry or the water.

'If we were meant to be on that side of the canal we'd have been born there,' they said, but Arkwright saw his chance and scrambled through the tangled branches to the opposite bank. Later on, when some of the others had changed their minds, it was too late. Men had come and taken the tree away and the bridge to freedom had gone. On calm nights Arkwright could still hear the others across the water fighting and squabbling.

He had been eleven years old when he had crossed the canal and now he was fifteen. He had had four good years, with plenty to eat and a warm dry home. In those years the house had been empty and Arkwright had lived in the cellar in an old rat's nest of warm newspapers. Away from the fighting and squabbling he had felt himself a king again. There were very few cats on this side of the water and those there were poor pampered creatures who avoided him. He had been lonely but he had felt at peace.

Then the people had moved into the house. They had closed up the hole into the cellar and Arkwright had spent the summer among the bushes and undergrowth. It had been a good summer, warm and well fed, but now winter had arrived and Arkwright began to feel his age. He was scared of people. He had seen the way they treated the cats around the factories and he knew man was something to keep away from, but the coal bunker was the only place he could find out of the biting wind.

At night he crept out into the garden to look for

food. He had a terrible pain in his front leg that made him walk with a slow limp, so slow that any thought of catching mice was out of the question. Soft yellow light shone from the house onto the lawn carrying with it the warm smell of food and the sound of laughing voices. Next door's cat was inside its house in the warmth by the fire, and Arkwright found himself wondering if maybe all humans weren't the same.

Maybe some of them are all right, he thought, but when he tried to follow next door's cat into its kitchen a thin woman threw a jug of water over him. A frost fell that night and the water froze in his fur and Arkwright lay in the coal bunker wishing he could just go quietly to sleep and never wake up again. But he didn't, he just sat in the coal dust and shivered until morning.

The frost stayed all day now and the people in the house turned up their new central heating and decided to light the fire. The man brushed away the leaves from the coal bunker lid and opened it. At first he didn't see the two yellow eyes staring up out of the blackness. Only when Arkwright ran limping out of the shute at the bottom did the man realise the cat was there. He called him, but of course Arkwright stayed hidden in the bushes.

When the old cat crept back to his shelter that night, there was a saucer just inside the door, a saucer of white liquid that Arkwright had never seen before, but he knew what it was.

'Poison,' he muttered.

He had seen dishes of it in the factories and seen what had happened to the rats and cats that had eaten it. Later that night a hedgehog stuck its nose in and drank the liquid. Arkwright thought he should warn the poor animal but whenever he'd said anything in the past they'd all cursed him.

Still, he thought, *I'm the only one who's lived past ten.* And then as the wind got colder he wondered if that had been such a great thing to achieve.

The next night the man put another saucer down and the hedgehog came back and emptied it.

'Was it you here last night?' said Arkwright.

'What if it was?' asked the hedgehog.

'Do you feel all right?' said Arkwright.

'What're you talking about?' said the hedgehog.

'The poison,' said Arkwright.

'What poison?'

'The poison in the saucer,' said Arkwright.

'That's not poison,' laughed the hedgehog. 'That's milk.' As soon as he'd said it he realised what an idiot he'd been. If he'd let Arkwright keep on believing the saucer was full of poison, he'd be able to come and drink it every night. Now the cat would get it.

And the cat did get it. He sat in the bushes until the man had gone back indoors and then he hurried over and drank every last drop. After two weeks he no longer bothered to hide. The man spoke gently to him as he put down the saucer and Arkwright's ancient fear began to soften. The man's children began to come too and they brought food as well as milk. They held out their small hands to Arkwright but he wasn't ready to touch them. A lifetime of avoiding man, and avoiding him with good reason, couldn't just vanish and although instinct drew him towards the children other older instincts from untamed ancestors kept him back. He was not a cat who had once been loved by humans and abandoned to go wild. He had been born wild to parents who had been wild.

As November became December Arkwright grew stronger. With food and drink each day he became fatter and his fur thickened against the cold. The children put a box with a cushion in it inside the coal bunker but still he wouldn't let them go near him. Every day when they came to feed him, they held out their hands and talked to him. Every day he sat at a safe distance and listened to them. He was unable to undertand the words but he felt from the way they spoke that they meant him no harm.

'Come on, cat,' said the boy, 'come and live in the house.'

'Come on, pussy,' said the girl, 'please.'

But Arkwright kept them at ten arms' lengths.

Although he was growing fatter and warmer, the arthritis in his front leg got no better. In fact it was getting worse. Sometimes the effort of walking hurt so much that he could barely move. The pain seemed to spread through his whole body even into the deepest corners of his brain. Only when he lay on his cushion and kept perfectly still did it get any better.

And that was how they caught him. The man came out with the saucer and as Arkwright tried to run away, the pain shot through him like a knife of fire and his leg collapsed beneath him. The man reached down and scooped him up and before he could spit or scratch he was in the house by the fire. For everyone there are times when they have to stop struggling, times when they have to shrug their shoulders and let things happen. For Arkwright it was that time. He saw the dancing flames of the fire, felt its sunshine sinking into his cold fur and realised that he had been cold for too long. The flames flickered and swayed in front of his eyes and, like humans and animals everywhere, he was hypnotised.

With the warmth of the house and the pills they gave him the pain in his leg grew less and less. For the rest of his life he walked with a limp but as long as he could jump up onto the little girl's bed he didn't care that he couldn't stalk mice. He lay in the soft quilt at the child's feet and dreamt of Gertrude.

If she could see me now, he thought, *what would she think?*

On Christmas day they gave Arkwright a collar. It was red velvet and had a medallion with his address on it.

I'm not going anywhere, he thought.

And he didn't, though when they started calling him Susie he did wonder about it.

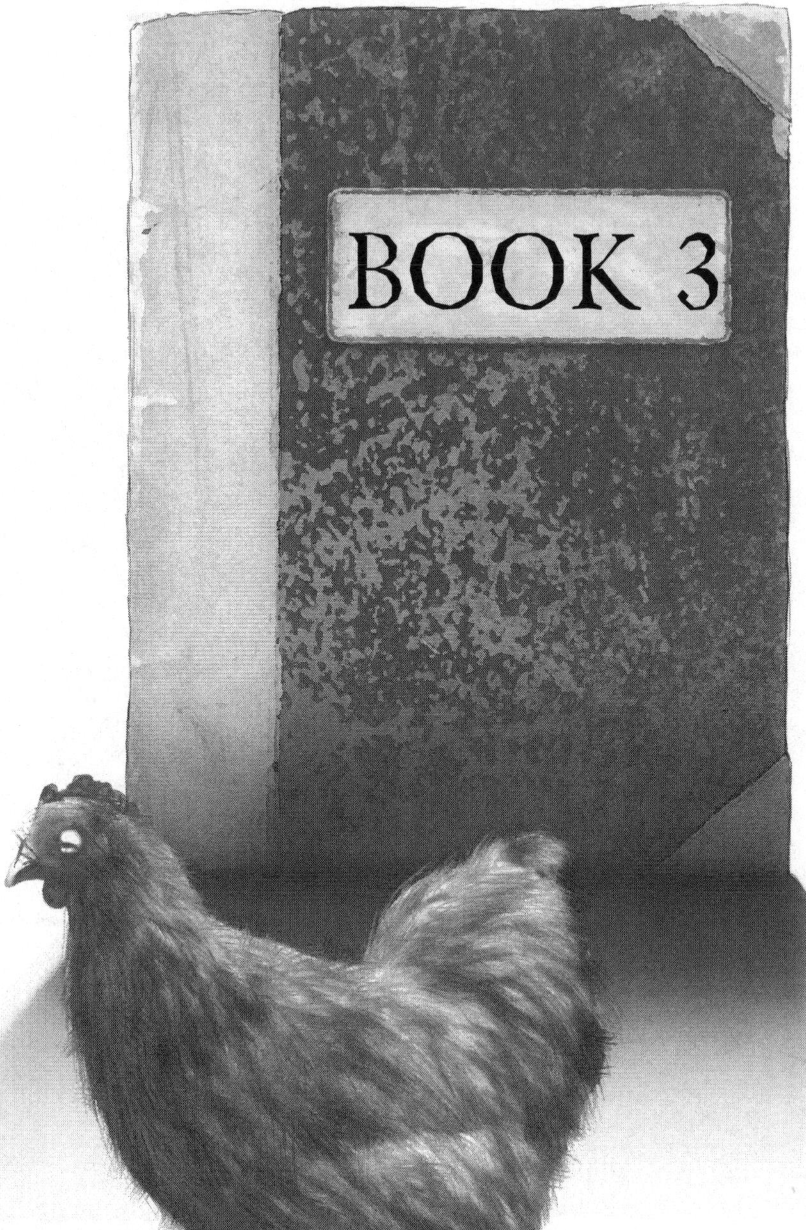
BOOK 3

Christmas

At the end of a quiet street, at the edge of a large town, stood a beautiful old house. On either side in flat silent gardens the houses sat cold and weary. There was heat inside them made by white boxes on kitchen walls that clicked and moaned through the winter nights, but outside the houses looked dull and lifeless. Their chimneys stood damp and empty above closed up fireplaces.

Only at the house called fourteen was it any different. The garden was like a sleeping jungle. It was the middle of winter. The leaves had fallen and the trees stood dark and quiet but still the garden was full of life. Birds cluttered up the branches and small secret creatures tunnelled through the thick piles of leaves hunting for food. The house itself looked warm and comfortable like a big armchair. There was no white box on its kitchen wall and in its fireplaces real fires danced and crackled. Every single brick was warm and cosy. The whole house seemed to glow in the November darkness.

The days of winter moved slowly on and it started

to get very cold. The sun kept low all day. Its light was weak and tired and gave out so little heat that the heavy frost lay undisturbed from dawn to dusk. Every twig, every blade of grass, was covered in crystals of ice that sparkled like a million tiny diamonds as the thin sun danced through them. A deep cold crept into every corner. In the deserted factories across the canal, ferns of ice crystals covered the windows and from the pale roofs icicles hung down towards the freezing ground. The canal itself froze over, dark dull grey at first then white as frost covered the surface. Ducks flew in sprawling and sliding across the ice, trailing wild skid marks and frantic footprints as they tried to slow down. As the swans came down they crashed into each other and sent the ducks scattering in all directions. For weeks the canal was covered with irritable clumsy birds falling down at every step yet too confused to fly away to warmer waters.

As the winter sank deeper and deeper into the earth so the worms and moles dug down below it. Sensible animals had flown away to warmer lands while those that were left did the best they could to survive. Some crept into their beds and hibernated. Others fluffed themselves up and waited for spring. People, unable to adapt like most animals, hid in thick clothes and blew clouds of steam into the air.

In December even the clouds grew cold and slipped quietly away. For two weeks the sky was pale blue from side to side. It was a thin wintery sky that seemed much less part of the world than the bright skies of summer. Far above, in its highest reaches, the smoke lines of aeroplanes crossed from one horizon to another covering the world in white cobwebs.

Dennis the owl sat in his big oak tree and shivered.

'I wish I could hibernate,' he said.

'Well, why don't you?' said a robin, sitting on a branch above him.

'I've tried,' said Dennis, 'but I keep falling asleep.'

'Yes, but . . .' the robin started to explain but Dennis wasn't listening. He was looking up at the sky. The sun had given up and gone off to Australia and thick black clouds were rolling across the town. It was as if someone was wrapping the world up in a heavy eiderdown. It was only midday but it had grown so dark that it felt like evening.

'Oh well,' said Dennis, 'time for bed.'

'Don't be silly,' said the robin. 'It's only midday.'

'But it's dark,' said Dennis. 'It must be bedtime.'

'It isn't always bedtime just because it's dark,' said the robin.

'Of course it is,' said Dennis.

'What about thunderstorms?' said the robin. 'The sky gets really dark when there's a thunderstorm. What do you do then?'

'Go to bed,' said Dennis and then he added, 'What do you do?'

'Hide under a branch until it's finished,' said the robin. 'And get wet.'

'That's clever,' said Dennis and went to bed.

Two days before Christmas it snowed. The wind stopped blowing, the bitter cold air seemed to grow warmer and at midnight the snow began to fall. The big white flakes floated down from the clouds in total silence. Other sounds grew fainter too. As the snow settled on the roads, the noise of the traffic grew softer. The whole city faded to a quiet murmur, quieter than the countryside. And beyond the city the countryside itself was as silent as an empty dream.

In the garden the animals that lived by night awoke to find their homes buried. The rabbits and the mice made new tunnels through the snow. Even though it was the first snow that many of them had seen, they knew by instinct what to do. Only Dennis the owl was confused. He hopped out of his hole in the oak tree and stood on the branch.

'Where's all the colour gone?' he said. 'It's washed away.'

Apart from the yellow squares of light from the windows across the lawn everything was white. Dennis walked along where he thought the branch should be and fell off. He floundered around on the ground kicking and flapping great clouds of snow into the air until he finally shook himself free and fluttered up to the tree.

'Help, I'm on fire,' he shouted. 'There's smoke everywhere.' But it was just the snow.

As daylight appeared the wind began to grow. The snow that had fallen as softly as feathers now began to dance in frantic circles. It grew until it was a blizzard running round and round the houses in a silent frenzy. It clung to walls and windows and piled itself up in great drifts against doors. Every animal fluffed itself up against the cold and waited. Birds sat huddled under branches while rabbits and mice peered out from their tunnels and watched nature's fury. It raged for hours until the whole world was painted white.

Inside the houses people slept. The snow on the windows blocked out the daylight so that all morning it was as dark as early dawn. Those who did wake up at the right time found it impossible to tell what time of day it was and others, waking late, looked at their watches in disbelief. Most of them, finding they were late for work, took the day off and went back to bed. The people who did try and travel found they couldn't get anywhere. The trains were frozen to the tracks, the buses locked up and cold and their cars wouldn't start. Nature gave the world a day off and as it was nearly Christmas no one really minded.

At the house called fourteen, the two children who lived there went out into the back garden and built a snowman. From inside his tree Dennis the owl watched wide-eyed as it grew taller and taller on the lawn.

'It'll end in tears,' he said, 'and they'll probably be mine.'

'For goodness sake, Dennis, stop twittering and go to sleep,' said Audrey the owl.

'But there's a huge giant on the lawn,' said Dennis.

Ethel the chicken stood in the doorway of the hen hut and looked out at the garden. She fluffed out her feathers and settled down in the straw. Sparrows were fluttering from branch to branch sending little gusts of snow tumbling down. The children had cleared the bird table and it seemed as if every bird for miles around was feeding there. The bluetits were fighting around the wire cages of peanuts and in the trampled snow below them clumsy pigeons were pecking up their crumbs.

At lunchtime the man came out and hung a long line of bright coloured lights across the bushes along the back of the house. Red, blue, green and yellow, at night they glowed in the darkness like big gentle eyes. Dennis thought it was the most beautiful thing he had ever seen.

'It looks like heaven has come down into the garden,' he said.

That night it snowed again, not great wild storms but just enough to fill in the footprints and smooth over the edges so that when everyone woke up on Christmas morning the world was new again. The snowman looked as if he had been wrapped up in a big flowing blanket. The roads that had become grey with traffic were clean and white again. The trees that had shrugged off their coats were covered once more and even the wires between the coloured lights had narrow snowdrifts balanced on them. It had frozen hard through the night and the pools of water where the sun had melted the snow the day before were now frozen through.

It was the first time in sixteen years that there had been snow on Christmas day. Of all the animals in the garden only Ethel was old enough to remember the last time. The two children hadn't even been born then and would probably have children of their own by the time it happened again. And even though the snow began to melt that afternoon, for the family at the house called fourteen it was the best Christmas they had ever known.

Winter Morning

In the dark before dawn
When the moon's crept away,
While the world is still sleeping,
Comes the first breath of day.

From beyond the horizon
Through the tall empty trees
The line of the sunshine
Drifts in with the breeze.

Shining light into windows
A ribbon of gold
Dances over the frost
Of a night grown old.

Then life wakes and stretches,
Crawls into the light,
Drawn out by old instincts
And the famine of night.

The frost beats the sun
And that's how it stays
And we'd rather be sleeping
Through Winter's cold days.

Four Pigeons

Steve and Raymond the pigeons sat on the gutter at the back of the house looking down into the garden. As they watched, a woman came out of the house and tipped some food onto the bird table. As soon as she turned away a crowd of sparrows and starlings flew down from the trees and began fighting and squabbling over the food. The noise was terrific with birds flapping and shouting at each other, pushing and shoving and swearing for all they were worth. Hardly had a bird got a single mouthful before it was being attacked by another.

'See that down there,' said Steve.

'What?' said his brother Raymond. Steve wasn't actually sure if Raymond was his brother or just another pigeon, but he thought they probably were brothers because they looked so alike. Raymond thought the opposite.

'That food,' said Steve.

'You're thick, you are,' said Raymond, for no apparent reason.

'Well, if I'm thick,' said Steve, 'then you're thicker.'

'Am not,' said Raymond.

'Are too,' said Steve.

'Not,' said Raymond.

'Are,' said Steve.

'Not.'

Steve said nothing for a bit and then threw himself at Raymond who fell off the gutter. The two birds flapped and crashed at each other until they landed on the bird table scaring all the other birds away.

'Look at all this food,' said Steve and started pecking away at a large currant bun with green mould on the edges.

'You're fat, you are,' said Raymond.

'Well, if I'm fat,' said Steve, 'then you're fatter.'

'Am not,' said Raymond.

'Are too,' said Steve.

'Not,' said Raymond.

'Are,' said Steve.

'Not.'

Steve pecked at his bun for a bit and then threw himself at Raymond who fell off the bird table. The two birds flapped and fought until they ended up in the bushes. The sparrows and starlings who had flown off when the pigeons had come crashing down went back to their own battle on the table and carried on with their breakfast.

The two pigeons fluttered out of the bush and sat on a branch getting their breath back.

'You're unhealthy, you are,' said Raymond, between taking deep breaths.

'Well, if I'm unhealthy,' puffed Steve, 'then you're unhealthier.'

'Am not,' said Raymond.

'Are too,' said Steve.

'Not,' said Raymond.

'Are,' said Steve.

'Not.'

Steve said nothing for a bit and then threw himself at Raymond who fell off the branch. The two birds fluttered at each other in the grass but they were so exhausted by now they could hardly hop off the ground.

'Do you ever get the feeling that this has all happened before?' said Raymond.

'No,' said Steve.

'Well, neither do I then,' said Raymond.

'I bet you do,' said Steve.

'Don't.'

'Well, why did you say it then?' said Steve.

'Er, because I thought you did,' said Raymond.

'Well, I don't,' said Steve.

Raymond crept under a twig and fluffed up his feathers. He shut his eyes and thought about sleeping. Steve stood and watched him and wondered how they could be so different. He was slim and clever while Raymond was fat and stupid. He was cool and handsome while Raymond was angry and ugly. It was amazing how unlike two brothers could be.

Raymond wondered how two pigeons could be so different. He was clever and slim while Steve was stupid and fat. He was handsome and cool while

Steve was ugly and angry. It was obvious that there was no way they could be brothers.

'What was your mother called?' he said.

'Mum,' said Steve.

'Liar,' said Raymond. 'That's what my mother was called.'

'Well, we're brothers,' said Steve. 'We've got the same mother.'

'Don't be ridiculous,' said Raymond. 'Look how different you are from me.'

'Well, if I'm different,' said Steve, 'then you're differenter.'

'Am not,' said Raymond.

'Are too,' said Steve.

'Not,' said Raymond.

'Are,' said Steve.

'Not.'

Steve said nothing for a bit and then fell over.

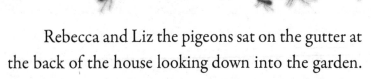

Rebecca and Liz the pigeons sat on the gutter at the back of the house looking down into the garden. There were two other pigeons fighting on the lawn.

They puffed out their chests and flapped at each other like a couple of over-stuffed cushions.

'See that down there?' said Rebecca.

'What?' said Liz.

'Those two idiots down there,' said Rebecca.

'How long have you had that bald patch?' said Liz.

'What bald patch?' said Rebecca. 'I haven't got a bald patch.'

'Yes, you have,' said Liz. 'On the back of your head.'

'Well, if I'm bald,' said Rebecca, 'then you're balder.'

'Am not,' said Liz.

'Are too,' said Rebecca.

'Not,' said Liz.

'Are,' said Rebecca.

'Not.'

Rebecca said nothing for a bit and then threw herself at Liz who fell off the gutter. The two birds flapped and crashed at each other until they landed on the bird table scaring all the other birds away.

'Look at all this food,' said Rebecca and started pecking away at a brown potato.

'You're fat, you are,' said Liz.

'I know,' said Rebecca. 'I'm much fatter than you.'

'Are not,' said Liz.

'Am too,' said Rebecca.

'Not,' said Liz.

'Am,' said Rebecca.

'Not.'

Rebecca pecked at her potato for a bit and then threw herself at Liz who fell off the bird table. The two birds flapped and fought until they ended up in the bushes. The sparrows and starlings who had flown off when the pigeons had come crashing down, went back to their own battle on the table and carried on with their breakfast.

The two pigeons fluttered out of the bush and sat on a branch getting their breath back.

'Hey, girls,' said Raymond. 'Come on now. You're behaving like a couple of kids.'

'Yeah,' said Steve, 'that's no way for ladies to carry on.'

'What!' exclaimed Rebecca. 'And what do you two think you've been doing for the last half an hour?'

'What are you talking about?' said Raymond.

'You two,' said Liz. 'You've been at it like a couple of stupid kids.'

'Have not,' said Steve.

'Have too,' said Liz.

'Have not,' said Raymond.

'Have,' said Rebecca.

'Not.'

Liz and Rebecca said nothing for a bit and then threw themselves at Raymond and Steve. The four birds jumped at each other, puffing themselves up as big as they could and calling each other every rude name they could think of. Rabbits covered their children's ears as they hurried by and ants ran for their lives. Feathers flew everywhere until at last the four birds stood exhausted and panting in a circle of trampled grass.

'Let that be a lesson to you,' said Steve.

'Yeah,' said Raymond. 'Just you watch it or we'll sort you out again.'

'You sort us out,' laughed Liz. 'Get real.'

'Come on, girls,' said Steve. 'Be honest, we won.'

'Yeah,' said Raymond. 'We let you off because you're girls.'

'You're unbelievable,' said Liz.

'Well, if we're unbelievable,' said Steve, 'then you're unbelievabler.'

'No such word,' said Rebecca.

'Is too,' said Steve.

'Isn't,' said Raymond.

'Is,' said Liz.

'Not.'

Steve and Raymond said nothing for a bit and fell over again. When they got up Rebecca and Liz had gone.

'Women, eh?' said Steve.

'Yeah,' said Raymond.

'Yeah.'

'Still, I thought the bald one was pretty,' said Raymond.

'Not as pretty as the other one,' said Steve.

'Was too,' said Raymond.

'Was not.'

'Was . . .'

Rosie

In the middle of nowhere it was as black as night. Rosie the puppy curled up into a pathetic little ball and tried to sleep. She was very cold and it was a long time since she had had anything to eat and all around her wild animals roared. Their noise was so loud that the ground shook beneath her. Rosie shook too not just from the cold but because for the first time in her short life she was completely terrified and alone.

She nuzzled around in the tiny darkness but there was no one there. Her brother and sisters and even her mother had all gone. She knew they wouldn't be there. She could still remember what had happened. One by one the others had been taken away until she had been the only one left. She had missed them terribly, missed the loving feel of them all rolling round together in the warm blanket; but then she had had her mother all to herself and for a few days it had been wonderful.

Rosie had been the smallest and the last to go. Someone had picked her up and suddenly it had all gone dark. That's how it was now, dark and alone. She had called out over and over again but no one had come.

The animals roared louder and high above them a terrible loud crash rolled across the world and it started to rain. A dull flash tried to light the darkness but the thunder chased it away. Rosie hid her face in her paws and shivered and the rain soaked through her fur, and very close in the night one great animal stopped and growled.

Across the motorway the rain came down in great thick curtains. The thunder was so loud that even inside the car with the engine racing they could hear it. Lightning flashed in brilliant sheets, lighting up the world so brightly that for a second the car's headlights were invisible. The red lights of other cars sparkled and flickered in the rain like distant fires.

The woman slowed down and pulled across to the inside lane and as she did so, the car slid sideways like a horse with a broken leg.

'What's the matter?' asked the girl from the back seat.

The woman pulled over onto the hard shoulder and stopped.

'I think we've got a puncture,' she said. They sat in the car as if by waiting everything would be all right. The engine ticked over so softly that in the storm no one could hear it. Only the windscreen wipers moved, waving backwards and forwards in a frantic attempt to clear away the rain. Cars and lorries crawled by, their tail lights winking at them as they slipped away into the darkness.

'I'm not going out in that,' said the woman. 'We'll wait for a bit, it's bound to ease off soon.' So they sat and waited and listened to the radio and outside a few inches from the flat tyre Rosie the puppy, tied up in a sack, grew weaker and weaker.

'Shall I go and have a look?' said the boy. 'See if we have got a puncture?'

'Okay,' said the woman.

The boy pulled his collar up and climbed out into the rain. The storm was moving away but it was still raining hard. He walked round the car looking at the wheels, then he climbed back in.

'It's the one at the front on the left,' he said.

When the rain had faded into a soft drizzle the woman and the boy got out and changed the wheel. Rosie had stopped moving. She was now no more than a wet rag like the sack she was imprisoned in. The boy stepped back and stood on the sack, barely a couple of inches from the tiny dog, but he never saw her. They put the flat wheel in the back of the car and the woman got back into the driving seat. It was only then, when the boy looked round for something to wipe his hands on, that he noticed the sack. He squatted down and cleaned his fingers and only then when he picked the sack up to throw it into the bushes, only then did it move.

'Come on, get back in the car,' said the woman, but the boy was on the ground pulling at the string.

'There's something here,' he said, 'in this sack.'

'Leave it alone,' said the woman. 'It could be anything.'

'But it's moving,' said the boy. 'It's something alive.'

The woman got out of the car and took the sack from the boy. She undid the string and lifted out the small wet dog. It lay still and pathetic in her hands, no larger than a kitten.

'I think it's dead,' she said and inside her, a giant anger brought tears to her eyes. She held the dead thing against her chest and stood there in the car's headlights as the rain began to fall heavily again. The tears poured down her face into the rain and washed away across the road. She looked up into the sky, up into the storm, and shouted at the top of her voice with a great wild desperate cry of fury. The boy took his mother's hand but there was nothing he could say. His mother's roar had said it all.

'We'll take it home and bury it in the garden,' the woman said. 'It's the least we can do.'

The boy took the tiny animal and put it inside his coat and they drove home in silence. The rain kept falling inside the car as badly as it was outside. The woman could hardly see to drive for her tears and on the back seat the two children sat sad and still. From time to time the woman cursed under her breath but apart from that none of them said a word until they were almost home.

It was past midnight when they left the motorway. Most people were in their beds and the streets were as empty as their hearts. The rain stopped and the clouds moved on, leaving a dark clear sky and inside the boy's coat the pitiful corpse grew warm, and right outside their house, it shook and shivered and the boy cried out and the woman turned round and drove the car right into the gatepost but it didn't matter.

Even the next morning, when Rosie was warm and dry and sleeping inside the boy's shirt, and they all went out and looked at the broken car, even then it didn't really matter. They mended the car but they left the gatepost to remind them of what had happened. They knew that whoever had been cruel enough to desert Rosie by the roadside had also thrown away all the years of happiness that she had to give, happiness that she would now give to them.

Ambrose the Cuckoo

Ambrose the cuckoo staggered about on the shed roof and tried to wake up. He'd just flown in from Africa and he was exhausted. As usual, he'd got lost and had ended up going the long way round. His head was buzzing, he was starving hungry and his wings were aching. He wasn't sure where he was or where he'd even come from. It might not have been Africa at all, it might have been Turkey or Mexico or none of those places. Wherever it was, it had been hot, very hot and now it was cold. And wherever it was, there had been cockroaches the size of rabbits, great big juicy delicious insects with soft succulent insides that were a meal all on their own. Now all there was were miserable worms and flies that moved too fast to catch.

It was the same every year. Some idiot would say: 'Hey guys, let's take a trip,' and like complete nitwits they did. They never learnt. It was great where they lived. The weather was always warm. It was true there was a lot of sand, hundreds of miles of it, to be honest; but there was always plenty to eat, big fat locusts by the million. It was always the same. As soon as they started flying north it began raining. If that wasn't bad enough, in some countries people tried to shoot them. It was always cold and there was never enough to eat. And to make things worse Ambrose was always the last to arrive and all the best nests were gone.

'Oh man,' said Ambrose, 'this cold is so uncool.' He hunched up his shoulders on the wet roof and shivered.

'It's the last time,' he said. 'Next year I'm staying at home.'

Another cuckoo landed on the shed and slid down the roof towards him. It was his wife Lola and she looked fed up; but then she always looked fed up.

Ambrose was not happy. Everything was so uncool.

'Three weeks I've been here,' said Lola. 'Three weeks waiting for Mr Cool to get here.'

'Oh man, just relax,' said Ambrose sliding slowly down the roof. He slid slowly into the gutter, got his feet all tangled up in rotten wet leaves and then toppled gently over the edge into a bush.

Far out, Ambrose thought, as he slipped down through the branches. *Time for bed.*

And he fell fast asleep. He didn't dream. He was too lazy to dream. He just lay on his back under the bush and snored, a weird noise that only a bird that can shout 'cuckoo' could make. Lola flew down and shouted at him but she knew that once Ambrose was asleep nothing would wake him.

'Great useless uncool lump,' she said and flew off to look for a nest.

It was the time of year when everyone was making or looking for nests. The garden had woken from a long winter. It had shivered through the early days of spring and now the promise of summer filled the air. New leaves flashed brilliant green, the grass began to grow, everyone woke up, and the birds that had been silent for months began to sing. Old visitors like the cuckoos and swallows, who had spent the winter in warmer places, were drifting back and inside the house the humans were spring cleaning.

The bluetits were clearing out last year's grass and moss, pulling it to bits and throwing it out. On the ground beneath them, mice were picking it up and using it for their nests. In the treetops pigeons and crows were pushing and poking fresh twigs into their old homes and inside the twigs themselves small insects were settling down to raise families.

Under the old garden shed the hedgehogs were waking up. They stretched and yawned and snuggled down into their beds of old newspapers. They knew it was time to get up but when you've been asleep for three months it takes a bit of time to wake up properly. Some of the young hedgehogs had been up and about for a week or more but the old ones needed at least a day to wake up properly.

Lola flew from tree to tree looking for the best place to lay her eggs. The pigeons and crows were too big and clumsy, they would just squash her eggs against their lumpy wooden nests. The bluetits were too clever, they built their nests in holes that were far too small for Lola to get in. There were no vacancies in the sparrows' nests. They'd either been taken already or their eggs had hatched. It was the same with the robin and the blackbirds. It happened like this every year. Ambrose was so lazy that everything was always left to the last minute. There was a wren's nest in one of the bushes but it was far too small and the starlings had built theirs in narrow gaps and holes.

The old chicken that had been there every year for as long as Lola could remember was ambling around through the undergrowth. She looked old and clumsy now but she had been in the garden longer than anyone.

She should know where all the nests are, thought Lola. *She must know every inch of the garden like the back of her foot.*

She flew down to talk to her.

'Well,' said Ethel when Lola asked her, 'I suppose you could borrow a bit of my nest.'

'Would you sit on one of my eggs for me?' said Lola.

'I'll sit on anything, dear,' said Ethel. 'At my age you can't afford to be fussy.'

It wasn't much of a choice but it was the only one she had. Ethel took her into the hen house and pointed at her nesting box. It was disgusting. It looked as if it hadn't been made for a week and there were bits of old sweaters and envelopes sticking out of the straw. A family of mice was living under one corner of it and there was a red hot-water bottle with a hole in it shoved down the back. And as for the smell, it was like something very old that had been left in a dark damp corner for a very long time. Which is exactly what it was.

'Is that it?' she said.

'Yes,' said Ethel proudly. 'Lovely, isn't it?'

'It's not exactly what I dreamt of,' said Lola.

'Please yourself,' said Ethel, starting to go back out into the garden.

'No, no,' said Lola, gritting her beak. 'It's lovely.' And closing her eyes and holding her breath she hopped into Ethel's nest and laid an egg.

'Bit small, isn't it?' said Ethel. 'But it's a nice colour.'

The old chicken climbed up into the mess of straw and paper and shuffled around until Lola's egg was buried deep in her chest feathers. She closed her eyes and sat clucking softly to herself. Soon she was snoring gently and far away in a land of dreams. Lola tiptoed to the door and flew away as quickly as she could.

The next morning when the children came down from the house to collect the eggs that Ethel's children had laid, they saw the old hen asleep in her nesting box and thought she was ill. She woke up when they spoke to her and when they offered her corn, she got up all stiff legged and clambered out onto the floor.

'Hey look, she's laid an egg,' said the boy.

'Small, isn't it?' said the girl.

'It's big enough for a tiny omelette,' said the boy and they put it in the basket with the other eggs.

Ethel ate her corn and went back to her nest for a nap. She was so old that she couldn't remember things like she'd used to and she didn't notice the egg had gone. She was all right with things that had happened a long time ago. They were just a bit fuzzy round the edges, but what had happened yesterday was different. When she tried to think about that she just ended up daydreaming.

After lunch Lola flew into the hut to see how things were going. She landed in front of Ethel and said, 'How's the egg?'

'Egg?' said Ethel. 'What egg?'

'My egg,' said Lola. 'The one I laid in your nest yesterday.'

'Oh, that egg,' said Ethel. 'What was it called?'

'Called?' said Lola. 'It wasn't called anything. You can't call them anything until they hatch out. You can't give them a name until you know if they're girls or boys.'

'The children did,' said Ethel. 'They gave it a name.'

'What name?' said Lola. 'What children?'

'The children who come and feed me,' said Ethel. 'They gave the egg a name.'

'Okay, okay, what did they call it?' sighed Lola. She knew something had happened to her egg. This was the price you paid for not having to build your own nest. Sometimes things went wrong and you had to start all over again.

'They called it Omelette,' said Ethel. 'Lovely name, isn't it?'

'Wake up, you great useless lump,' shouted Lola. Ambrose rolled over onto his side, blinked and slowly stood up. His feathers stood out at all angles, his claws were full of mud and his whole appearance made him look as if he had been pulled through a bush backwards, which is exactly what had happened.

'I'll have a large stick insect, man, and make it snappy,' he said. Lola shouted at him some more until at last he was as awake as he was ever going to be.

'Hey man,' he said with a stupid grin. 'How's it going?'

'Stop calling me man,' said Lola, 'and concentrate.'

'Cool,' said Ambrose, staring at his feet and sulking.

Lola told him what had happened, how she'd been all over the garden and been made to look a fool by the owls and what had happened to the egg she'd laid in Ethel's nest.

'It's getting very late,' she went on, 'and you've got to help me find a nest.'

'Far out, man,' said Ambrose.

'Never mind all that,' said Lola. 'You're usless in the air so you look on the ground while I check round all the bushes and trees.'

'Yeah, man,' said Ambrose. 'I'll groove around in the grass.'

'Go on then,' said Lola. 'Wipe that stupid grin off your face and get going.'

Ambrose ambled off towards the pond.

'And don't spend hours talking to your reflection,' Lola shouted after him when she saw where he was going.

Ambrose stared into the water and there was his beautiful reflection looking up at him. He was the handsomest bird he'd ever seen, so sleek, so colourful and above all, so cool.

'Hi there, handsome,' he said to himself. His reflection just sat there staring back at him with its eyes full of admiration.

Okay, Ambrose thought. *He's too cool to speak to me, but I can tell he thinks I'm cool too.*

'Will you shut up?' said a voice. 'Some of us are trying to lay eggs and all your useless chattering is putting us off.'

Ambrose looked up and there was an angry moorhen. She swam backwards and forwards in front of him making his beautiful reflection go all wobbly. And half-hidden in the long grass on the other side of the pond was her nest. It was wide and soft and had three eggs in it. It was perfect.

Oh wow, thought Ambrose and flew up into the trees to find Lola. He couldn't believe that he'd

246

actually done something clever and useful. Neither could Lola. It took Ambrose a long time to persuade her to go and look at the moorhen's nest but as soon as she did, she was delighted.

'Oh man,' she said. 'I take back all those nasty things I said about you. You're brilliant.'

So while Ambrose distracted the moorhen by singing to his shadow, Lola laid a big beautiful egg in its nest.

As the days passed, Lola and Ambrose hid in the treetops above the pond and kept an eye on things. Eventually her beautiful baby hatched out and while the moorhens' backs were turned it rolled the other eggs out of the nest into the water.

'Oh, look at him,' said Lola. 'He's so handsome, just like you.'

'Yeah, cool,' said Ambrose.

'He's grown so fast,' said Lola.

A few weeks later Ambrose and Lola set off back to Africa.

'If we go now,' said Lola, 'we'll miss the rush.'

For once Ambrose didn't argue with her. He missed the hot sunshine and giant cockroaches.

'What about our son?' he said, but already he

could see the endless African plains stretching out in his imagination.

'Oh, he'll be all right,' said Lola. 'He'll catch us up.'

And she was right. Their son was almost ready to follow them. The day after they left, when the moorhen swam away from her nest, the baby cuckoo followed her. He raised his tiny head to the sky, opened his bright red mouth and said, 'Cuckoooo... splutter... glug, glug, glug.'

Ffiona the Shrew

Ffiona the shrew was nervous. Not for any special reason, but because she was a shrew and shrews are always nervous. From the very second they are born to the day they die they are nervous. That's what being a shrew is all about, from the minute they wake up, until they fall asleep at night they are nervous. And even then it doesn't stop, because in their dreams they are nervous too. Other animals, and people too, do wild and wonderful things in their dreams but not shrews. They just dream about more ways of being scared.

'Not that I dream very often,' said Ffiona.

'Why not?' said her sister Jjoice.

'I'm too nervous,' said Ffiona.

'What, too nervous to dream?' said Jjoice.

'No, too nervous to go to sleep,' said Ffiona.

'Well, we're all nervous, dear,' said her brother Ssamson. 'That's what being a shrew is all about.'

'Well, it's hardly suprising,' said Ffiona. 'I mean, well, I mean, look at all the awful things there are in the world.'

'Like what?' said Ssamson.

'All the noise, all that stuff,' said Ffiona. 'All the roar of the grass growing and the flowers opening.'

'My goodness,' said the other shrews. 'You really are nervous.'

'Even more nervous than my Great Uncle Nernernornorman,' said Jjoice, 'and he was frightened of his own fur. He thought it would grow so long while he was asleep that it would suffocate him.'

'He was quite right,' said Ffiona. 'You have to be careful how you curl up too, or else your tail might strangle you.'

'Oh, come on,' said Bbasil. 'Get real.'

Bbasil wasn't like the other shrews. By comparison to them he was brave and fearless. Bbasil had been to the end of the garden and he had been inside a paper bag with his eyes open. Bbasil was a legend among shrews and naturally all the others were nervous of him. Bbasil was so brave he was even thinking of calling himself Basil.

'It's true,' said Ffiona. 'My aunt Ddaisy was killed by her own claws. She fell asleep somewhere too warm and they grew so fast they stabbed her to death before she could wake up.'

'Rubbish,' said Bbasil.

'It's not. It's true,' said Ffiona. 'My mum told . . . oh, oh, what's that?'

Ffiona ran into the darkest corner of the tunnel and hid her eyes.

'What?'

'That terrible roaring noise,' said Ffiona. 'It's a dreadful monster coming to get us.'

'No,' said Bbasil. 'It's someone in the house flushing the toilet.'

'Oh, oh, the toilet's coming to get us,' cried Ffiona. 'We're all going to die.'

It was the same every day, there was always something menacing going on. If it wasn't huge noisy leaves crashing down onto the lawn, it was some butterfly flapping its wings together in a threatening way. Ffiona couldn't understand how they survived at all with everything and everyone in the world trying to get them. When it snowed she thought they'd all be suffocated. When it rained she thought they'd all be drowned and when the sun came out she thought they all be cooked.

'It didn't used to be like this,' she said. 'Two weeks ago, when I was young, it was peaceful and safe. It's this terrible modern world we live in.'

'That's not true,' said Ssamson. 'I've been frightened from the minute I was born.'

'Yes, you're right,' said Ffiona. 'So have I. I was just too scared to remember it.'

'Well, I'm not frightened of anything, not even the dark,' said Bbasil and to prove it he closed his eyes.

'Don't do that,' said Ffiona. 'It's terrifying.'

'Oh yeah, well, I'm not scared at all,' said Bbasil and he walked straight into the wall.

He wasn't scared but he was incredibly stupid. With his ears ringing, he staggered along the tunnel and out into the daylight. The bright sun hit his face and dazzled him. He walked round and round in circles until he tripped over a pebble and fell straight down a deep drain.

Later on when she heard the news Ffiona would have said, if she hadn't been too scared to, that maybe being scared wasn't such a bad thing after all.

'After all,' said Jjoice, 'if Bbasil had been scared he'd still be here today.'

And she was right because the other shrews led full, happy and terrified lives and all lived to the ripe old age of four weeks.

Joey the Budgerigar

Joey the budgerigar sat on the top of the open window and looked out into the sunshine. Behind him an anxious human voice told him to sit perfectly still but in front of him a stronger voice coaxed him out into a world he had never known.

'Joey, good boy, there's a good boy,' said the human voice. 'Sit still for mummy.'

'Joey, come on,' said the voice inside his head. 'Fly away.'

The warm sun shone on his soft blue chest. The air smelt sweet and thick with the flowers of summer. Behind him the frightened voice of the woman who had loved him for as long as he could remember, talked softly to him. There were tears in her voice but the call of freedom was too strong to resist and Joey threw himself into the garden. He fluttered down towards the lawn but before he reached it he flapped his wings and soared up into the open sky.

Higher and higher he flew, a bright blue flash against a bright blue sky, until his wings ached like they had never ached before. Once a week he had flown round the room while his owner had cleaned his cage. Once a week he had flapped from the chair to the curtains, from the curtains to the sideboard and then back to his cage. Apart from attacking his reflection in his mirror that was all the exercise he had ever had. And now there were no bars any more. Now he was free.

He looked down at the house he had escaped from. In the back garden the woman who had kept him imprisoned all those years was running round her garden calling his name. Joey flew down into the top of a tall tree in the next garden and rested. Everywhere was so big that he couldn't take it all in. As far as he could see in any direction there was more and more to look at. It just seemed to go on forever with no walls or doors or windows anywhere.

I wonder where they hang their pictures, he thought.

'Hello, Joey,' he said. 'Who's a pretty boy?'

Below him in the wild garden some sparrows were hopping about in the grass pecking up seeds so Joey flew down to see them. At first they took no notice of him but after he'd asked them who was a pretty boy for the fiftieth time they could ignore him no longer.

'Well, not you,' said one of the sparrows.

'Yes,' said another. 'Who ever heard of a bird that was coloured blue?'

'What?' said Joey. 'Hello, Joey. Who's a pretty boy?'

'What's the matter with him?' said the first sparrow. 'Is he a bit simple?'

'Joey's a clever boy,' said Joey.

'Maybe he fell in a tin of blue paint and swallowed some,' said a third sparrow.

'Hello, Joey,' said the poor confused budgie. 'Someone at the door, someone at the door.'

'I think we should attack him,' said one of the

sparrows. 'That's what sparrows do to strange birds, isn't it?'

'Only if they're smaller than us,' said the first sparrow. 'I'm not going near him, not with that beak.'

'Time for Joey's bath. Joey's a clever boy,' said Joey and jumped into Rosie the dog's water bowl. This wouldn't have been too bad except that Rosie was asleep in the grass right next to her water bowl and Joey's vigorous splashing soon woke her up. The sparrows flew off to the bottom of the garden as Rosie stood up and shook herself.

'Hello, Joey,' said the wet budgie, hopping out of the water.

Rosie leant forward and sniffed Joey. He was the most beautiful bird she had ever seen, as blue as the sky, just like a dream.

'Woof, woof,' said Joey.

'What?' said Rosie.

'Sorry,' said Joey, 'it's a habit. I imitate everyone.'

'Gosh, that's clever,' said Rosie. 'Who were you doing then?'

'When?'

'When you said woof, woof?' said Rosie.

'You,' said Joey. 'Joey's a clever boy. Time for Joey's bath.'

'Woof, woof?' said Rosie. 'I don't say woof, woof.'

Joey explained that was how dogs sounded to humans.

'No, no,' said Rosie, 'that's wrong. That's how humans sound to dogs.'

'No, you've got it the wrong way round,' said Joey. ' Humans say tweet, tweet all the time.'

'Can we talk about something else?' said Rosie.

Just then Joey's human put her head over the fence and pleaded softly and gently with him.

'Come to mummy, there's a good boy,' she said. 'Come to mummy.'

'See,' said Joey. 'I told you they say tweet, tweet, tweet.'

'That one didn't,' said Rosie. 'She just said woof, woof, woof.'

As soon as Rosie spoke, Joey's human jumped up and down behind the fence and waved her hands around.

'Help, help,' she screamed. 'That awful dog's going to eat my baby.'

'Tweet, tweet,' shouted Joey and flew into the bushes.

'Woof, woof,' shouted Rosie and ran after her.

'Oh, my precious baby,' cried Joey's human and ran off into her house.

'Who on earth's that awful woman?' said Rosie. 'She whinges a lot, doesn't she?'

'She used to keep me inside her house, locked up in a tiny cage,' said Joey.

'That's awful,' said Rosie. 'Nobody should be locked up.'

'I know,' said Joey. 'I used to sit at the bars and look out into the garden and feel so lonely.'

'Well, you don't have to be lonely now,' said Rosie. 'I'll be your friend.'

'Woof, woof,' said Joey.

'Tweet, tweet,' said Rosie.

'Still, it wasn't all bad,' said Joey. 'I had a lovely mirror.'

The back door of the house opened and the two children and Joey's owner came rushing out. They ran around the lawn looking into the bushes and up through the branches. Rosie ran out into the open to distract them while Joey flew down and hid in the thick brambles by the canal.

'Oh, oh,' Joey's owner cried. 'Your horrible little dog's eaten my beautiful baby.'

Joey heard her and flew back across the lawn in case her new friend got into trouble. He flew up and landed on the gutter and looked down at them.

'Who's a pretty boy?' he called out, just in case they hadn't seen him.

'There he is,' shouted the children.

'Joey's a clever boy,' said Joey.

'Joey, come to mummy, there's a good boy,' she said. 'Come to mummy.'

The children tried to hide their grinning faces from the woman. She sounded so stupid and they felt quite sorry for Joey. Rosie ran round and round barking and jumping in the air. The children's mother came out but she had no more sympathy for the woman than her children. Everyone at the house called fourteen was definitely on Joey's side. They didn't like animals being locked up and they weren't going to change their minds for Joey's owner.

'You just go home,' said the children's mother, 'and we'll see if we can lure him into the house with a nice bit of cuttlefish.'

'Cuttlefish, I'm sick to death of cuttlefish,' said Joey when he saw it sitting on the kitchen window sill. 'Who ever got the idea that budgerigars like cuttlefish? What do they think we do, deep-sea dive for it, swim under water with a sharp knife and kill squid?'

'Yeah,' said Rosie. 'Quite right. What's a cuttlefish?'

Joey spent the rest of the afternoon flying around the garden eating things. After a lifetime of eating the same old boring bird seed every single day, it was like being in a giant supermarket. There was so much to choose from. At first he followed the other birds and ate what they were eating. While it meant eating grass seeds and peanuts in the bird feeder, it was all right, everything tasted wonderful, fresh and exciting. When it meant poking about in the grass for slugs, he wasn't quite so sure about it. His beak was the wrong shape and all he got was mouthfuls of mud. When he finally did manage to eat a slug, he decided the mud was better. It took a lot of drinking and spitting in the pond to get rid of the awful slimy taste.

He drove all the other birds mad with his endless chattering. It wasn't just that they hadn't the faintest idea what he was talking about, it was more that he kept saying the same thing over and over again. By the end of the day every single animal in the garden knew that he was a pretty boy, he was a clever boy and that there was someone at the door.

'I don't care how dangerous his beak looks,' said one of the sparrows. 'If he tells me once more what a pretty boy he is, I'll kill him.'

'Yeah,' said another. 'He's driving me mad.'

'Maybe we could get the cuckoos to have a go at him,' said a third.

'No, they like him,' said the first sparrow. 'Every time they go near him, he just imitates them.'

As dusk fell all the animals began to go to their beds. Rosie went indoors for her supper and then curled up on someone's lap. The sparrows that weren't sitting on eggs perched on branches next to their nests and one by one most of the other birds settled down for the night. A family of swans out on the canal floated slowly through the water, their long necks curved gracefully round as they tucked their heads back under their wings and slept. Only the owls were different. For them it was time to wake up. Other animals were beginning their days too. The rabbits came to the mouths of their burrows and sniffed the air, while the hedgehogs scrambled out from under the shed and began to crash about through the long grass. Everyone had somewhere to go. Everyone, that is, except Joey.

Joey had never really seen the night before. Sometimes when his owner had forgotten to close the curtains he'd sat in his cage and looked out at the darkening sky, but there had always been a light on in the room. Outside the window had just been like looking at a painting. Now he was inside that painting and he didn't know what to do. It was getting cold too and that was something Joey had never felt before.

As the sun set, the shape of the trees grew sharp against the dark gold sky. The leaves and branches changed from green and brown to deep black and Joey felt his beak begin to chatter. He fluffed up his feathers and flew from branch to branch but no one wanted him. Everyone had their place and Joey's place was next door in a chromium cage.

'Go away,' said the sparrows.

'There's no room here,' said the blackbirds.

'This is private property,' said the robin.

'Ooh, breakfast,' said Dennis the owl. 'I've never had blue breakfast before.'

The sky grew darker until the only light was the warm gold glow from the house windows. Great dark clouds rolled across the sky covering the moon and stars. Joey flew down onto the lawn and stood in the pool of light from the French windows. And as he stood there it began to rain.

'Not time for Joey's bath,' he said as the cold water soaked through to his skin.

'You look wet,' said a terrifying round prickly thing. It was Barry the hedgehog. Joey had never seen a hedgehog and thought Barry was the weirdest looking creature he'd ever seen.

'Are you a nightmare?' he said, shivering with cold and fear.

'No, of course not,' said Barry. 'I'm a hedgehog and if you stand out here in the pouring rain, you'll either die of cold or the owls will get you.'

'I've got nowhere to go,' said Joey. 'Everyone keeps chasing me away.'

'Follow me,' said Barry. 'I know someone who'll look after you.'

Barry walked across the lawn towards the bottom

of the garden and Joey walked slowly after him. The hedgehog had to keep waiting for the wet budgerigar to catch up because the bird could hardly see in the darkness. When they reached the chicken hut, Barry went inside and across to Ethel's nest. The old chicken was sitting fluffed up staring into the darkness.

'I just don't seem to be able to get to sleep any more,' she said.

Barry told her what had happened and Ethel was only too happy to help.

'I've sat on all sorts of things in my time,' she said, 'but never a blue bird.'

Joey hopped up into Ethel's nesting box and the old chicken tucked him under her wing. He told her everything that had happened since his escape that morning, how wonderful it had felt to be free, but how it had all changed when night had fallen.

'What I can't understand,' said Ethel, 'is why you want to be free. I certainly don't.'

'But you are free,' said Joey. 'You can go wherever you like and you can do whatever you feel like doing.'

'But I don't,' said Ethel, 'and I don't want to. I want to belong to someone. I like knowing that there are people who will look after me.' And she told Joey about the time when the house had been deserted and how lonely she had felt.

'I mean, everyone's nice to you, aren't they?' she said.

'Oh yes,' said Joey, 'I get food and water every day and I've got a lovely mirror with another budgie in it just like me and when I sing to him, he sings to me.'

'Well then,' said Ethel.

'Yes, but I'm not free,' said Joey.

'To do what?' said Ethel. 'Get soaked through and eaten by owls?'

'Yes,' said Joey. 'Well, err, no.'

They talked on and on until the morning and Joey knew, as he had done from the start really, that being free was as much about how you felt inside your head as it was about flying through the trees. Like the swans belonged on the river and the sparrows belonged in the trees, so Joey knew that he belonged next door in a shiny silver cage with a beautiful mirror and a lovely piece of cuttlefish. He'd been in the trees. He'd had a wonderful adventure but now it was time to go home.

He flew out of the chicken hut up into the sky as far as he could go. The world was waking up and the air was still cold with the chill of night. Down below he could see his home and it looked safe and inviting. He wanted to say goodbye to Rosie but there was no sign of her as he flew down into the trees in the wild garden.

The window next door was open, the window he had flown out of the day before.

'Joey, come on,' said a voice inside his head. 'Come home.'

And he did.

Godfrey the Maggot

Godfrey the maggot ate his way deeper into the peach. All around him everything was soft and wet and golden. Behind him a warm breeze tickled his back but as he tunnelled deeper into the fruit the air grew cool and still. He had been eating his way backwards and forwards through the peach for his whole life, all three days of it. In that time he had seen the whole world from the bright light shining through the skin to the dark mysteries of the centre with its magnificent stone. In all that time he had never seen another living soul. Every day he grew fatter and happier and the tunnels he made grew wider and

268

wider. The whole peach was all his and he felt pretty pleased and important.

'Life is completely brilliant,' he said. 'How many animals can eat their own homes?'

He ate a bit more and then said, 'I mean, you don't even have to get out of bed for breakfast. You just eat your bed.'

'You don't half talk a lot,' said a voice behind him.

Godfrey jumped so hard that he banged his head. He tried to see where the voice was coming from but the tunnel was no wider than he was so he couldn't. By the time he had eaten a space big enough and turned round, the owner of the voice had gone. All Godfrey could see was another tunnel cutting right across his own. He looked down it but it was quite empty. He ate himself back round again and carried on the way he had been going. In front of him it grew lighter and Godfrey knew he was reaching the other side of the peach again. He started eating an extra mouthful to the right each time and gradually began to turn back towards the middle.

'Round we go,' he said. 'Round we go.'

'Don't you ever stop talking?' said the voice behind him again.

Once again Godfrey ate a space to turn round in and once again there was no one there, just the tunnel crossing his own. He turned back and carried on.

'I'll keep really quiet,' he said to himself. 'Really, really quiet and then I'll catch him.'

As he got near the centre of the world he crossed another tunnel, but instead of going by, he went down it.

If I go really fast, he thought, *I'll catch up with him.*

He wriggled down the tunnel as fast as he could. It was a strange feeling, not eating, and Godfrey began to feel uncomfortable. The tunnel stretched ahead of him in a long curve that never seemed to end. He shut his eyes and wriggled faster and faster until he came to a sudden end and smashed his head against the peach stone. Maggots don't have hard things in their heads like skulls, so when they bang their heads, their brains wobble around like frightened jellies. Godfrey would have seen stars if he had known what they were but as all he had ever seen was fruit that was what he saw. His head spun and he saw fruit.

'You're stupid as well as noisy,' laughed the voice behind him. Godfrey spun round and saw the back end of another maggot wriggling off down the tunnel.

This went on for several days and as it did so Godfrey felt the peach begin to get softer. The juice was becoming a problem too. At first he could just drink it but now the tunnels were running wet and sticky. With every bite the whole place got wetter and wetter. In some places the tunnels were completely flooded and Godfrey had to eat through soft brown patches that tasted awful and collapsed around him.

'It's the end of the world,' he said.

'It's time to pupate,' said the voice but this time it was right in front of him. There looking straight at him was himself, or what he imagined himself to look like.

'Who are you?' he said.

'Godfrey,' said the other maggot.

'But I'm Godfrey,' said Godfrey.

'We all are,' said twenty other maggots that had appeared from various tunnels.

'Yes, and we better get out of here, quickly,' said the first stranger, 'before this whole thing comes crashing down around us.'

The twenty-two fat maggots bit their way through the peach skin and crawled out bleary-eyed into the sunshine. Above their heads the golden light danced and sparkled through the nettle leaves. Below them the grass shone like a soft quilt. It was the most beautiful sight they had ever seen.

'Is this heaven?' said the first Godfrey.

'I think it must be,' said one of the others.

They all thought it was heaven and so did the happy blue budgerigar as it ate twenty-two fat juicy maggots for breakfast.

Bert the Crow

Bert the crow sat in the top of the tallest tree in the garden and looked down through the branches. It was a beautiful spring day. The buds were starting to open but the leaves were still small enough to give a clear view down into the garden. On the lawn, the soft round shape of Ethel the chicken waddled slowly about pecking between the blades of grass. Even so far above ground Bert could see the slugs and worms as they sparkled in the sunlight. He had been out on the motorway all morning and although the slugs looked particularly tasty in the midday sun, Bert couldn't have eaten another mouthful.

'What was that you were eating this morning, our Bert?' said his mother.

'I haven't the faintest idea, Mother,' said Bert. 'It was black. I know that.'

'Fur or feathers?' asked his mother.

'Fur, I think,' said Bert. 'I was too busy dodging the cars to pay much attention.'

'True enough, lad,' said Bert's dad. 'The roads were right busy this morning.'

'I'll tell you one thing, though,' said Bert. 'Whatever it was I was eating, it was right flat.'

'Aye, lad,' said his father. 'It were dead flat.' And they all laughed.

'The flatter the better, I reckon,' said Bert. 'There's nothing like a few heavy lorries rolling over it to make your dinner nice and tender.'

'True enough, lad,' said Bert's dad. 'The heavier the better.'

'Tell us about the two-metre hedgehog, our dad,' said Bert's mum. 'You know, the one the railway engine ran over.'

'Nay, lass, it was a huge eighty-four-wheeler lorry with a train on the back, what did it,' said Bert's dad. 'That poor hedgehog was over two metres long and it was so flat you could see daylight through it.'

'Was it flatter than that squirrel we had on Sunday?' asked Bert.

'Oh aye, lad,' said Bert's dad. 'That squirrel was like Mount Everest compared to the two-metre hedgehog. Why, it was so thin it rustled in the breeze.'

'Eeee,' said Bert's mum.

'Aye,' said Bert's dad.

'What did it look like, Dad?' said Bert. 'Could you read a book through it?'

'Well, I never actually saw it myself, lad,' said Bert's dad, 'but I'm sure you could.'

Bert's dad didn't actually know what a book was but he wasn't going to let Bert know that.

The three crows sat in the afternoon sunshine and day-dreamed. Bert's mum dreamt about the old days when the factories across the canal had been a hive of activity. Big lorries with fat tyres had been in and out all day long and food had been plentiful and flat. Bert dreamt of finding the flattest widest meal there had ever been, a meal that was spread so thin you could hardly see it, a meal that would make the two-metre hedgehog look like a door mat. And Bert's dad just sat with his eyes closed and hoped no one would find out that the two-metre hedgehog was just a story his father had told him when he was a little fledgling. It had been an old story then. His father had heard it from his grandfather and one day Bert's dad supposed he would have to tell Bert that it was just a story, but not yet.

'Those were the days,' said Bert's mum.

'Aye, lass,' said Bert's dad. 'The flat old days.'

The days were really beginning to feel warm again now. There had been a time in the middle of winter when it seemed as if it would be cold forever, but now you could tell that summer was on its way. The two older crows turned their faces up to the warmth of the sunshine and soon fell fast asleep.

Bert was bored. He didn't want to sit around all afternoon. He kept thinking about the two-metre hedgehog. He tried to imagine how it must have tasted. To us the thought of a poor hedgehog rolled out like a table cloth is rather horrible but to Bert it seemed as delicious as a strawberry tart covered in thick cream and custard and chocolate flakes and fudge sauce and sugar.

He flew up above the house and out across the canal to the factories on the far side. Most of them were deserted now, with broken windows and rusting steel roofs. There were weeds growing up through the split concrete where cars and lorries had once parked. Inside the old buildings the air was still and silent. The machines and desks had been taken away years before and all that was left now were rusty marks on dusty floors and faded yellow notices pinned to peeling doors. Mice and spiders were the kings and queens in this forgotten landscape. A few birds nested in broken walls. Half-starved, half-wild cats roamed the corridors hunting half-starved rats and the occasional fox passed through but there was nothing there for crows.

There were still a few factories working. They looked almost as tired as the ones that were closed down and there were no big lorries anywhere to squash something juicy with. There were a few cars and a couple of fork lift trucks but that was about it. There was nothing moving that would squash anything really flat.

Bert flew on beyond the industrial estate, past the three-hundred-foot-tall chimney. There were a lot of big machines parked on some empty land but none of them were moving and beyond that there were just more houses. As it started to get dark he turned for home. His parents were still sitting on the gutter at the back of the house, still muttering away in their daydreams. Bert flew into the tall tree where they all roosted and fell asleep.

The next morning a passing crow told them about the new roadworks that had started by the old chimney.

'And we all know what that means, don't we?' said the visitor.

'Aye, lad,' said Bert's dad. 'Lots of big machines, lots of big fat heavy tyres to squash things.'

'Aye, breakfast,' said Bert's mum.

For the next few months there was plenty to eat and everyone grew fat and happy. Bert's mum hatched out four new eggs and was busy all day feeding them. Bert spent every day, until it was almost too dark to see, hanging round the roadworks with a gang of other crows. Sometimes there was so much great flat stuff to eat it was too dark to get home by the time they'd finished and they'd all spend the night inside the three-hundred-foot chimney.

But all the time Bert couldn't get the thought of the two-metre hedgehog out of his mind. He told his mates about the two-metre hedgehog but they all seemed to know about it already.

'It's just a story,' said Eddie. Eddie was a flash bird from the roughest part of town and all the others were a bit afraid of him. If you had any sense you didn't argue with Eddie.

'Are you sure?' said Bert. 'My dad reckons it's true.'

'Yeah, well, so does my dad,' said Eddie, 'but he's never seen it.'

'No, neither has mine,' said Bert.

'I reckon it's all made up,' said Eddie.

'You're probably right,' said Bert.

Bert couldn't really believe that Eddie was right. To do that would mean he'd have to say his dad had lied to him and he couldn't imagine him ever doing that.

Eddie's dad probably just heard about it from someone who had told someone else about someone who had heard it from his cousin's uncle's friend, he thought. *That's why Eddie doesn't believe it.*

The roadworks were coming to an end but that was the best time. That was the time they brought in the steam-rollers and then things got really flat. Not many things got squashed but when they did they were the sweetest things any of them had ever tasted. Bert's flattest meal was pink, or rather it had started off pink but by the time Bert got it it was a dirty grey colour.

The steam-roller driver had spat it out onto the fresh black tarmac as he had climbed up into the cab and then he'd driven over it. Bert had seen it but when the machine had passed it had vanished. At first he thought someone else had got it, but the others had gone to the station for the day to scavenge round the trains. He looked all over the road but the pink stuff had gone. He looked after the roller and there it was, stuck to the great steel front wheel and every time the machine rolled forward the pink stuff got flatter and flatter.

Bert hopped after the steam-roller all morning watching the amazing meal get wider and thinner with every turn. When the machine stopped for lunch it had got so thin and picked up so much dirt that it was almost invisible.

'Oh wow,' said Bert. 'It must be a million times thinner than the two-metre hedgehog.'

And it was but when he pecked and peeled it off

the wheel it was awful. It collapsed into a disgusting wriggling mess that stuck to his feathers and glued his beak together.

'Ee look, our dad,' said Bert's mum. 'Our Bert's got his first chewing gum.'

'Aye, lass, that takes me back,' said Bert's dad.

'Flat enough for you, is it?' said Bert's mum and the two crows fell out of the tree from laughing.

'Nnnnn . . . nnnn thh,' said Bert, scraping his beak along the branch over and over again.

It was two days before he finally got rid of the last of it and by then he was starving. He flew back to the roadworks but everything was gone. There was one small van and a few men poking around near the three-hundred-foot chimney but all the big machines were gone.

'I'm so hungry,' Bert said to himself, 'that I could eat something fat.'

He sat on top of the chimney and peered down and there far below at the foot of the tower was a tiny white speck. Bert slid off the ledge and floated down towards it. There, lying in the grass, was a big thick ham sandwich. As he got near the ground a rat crawled out from a gap in the bricks and grabbed the sandwich. It chewed and tore at it and tried to pull it into the gap but before it could and before Bert could reach it, the whole world exploded with the greatest explosion anyone had ever heard.

Bert was thrown outwards as the whole tower came crashing down on itself. In a great cloud of bricks and dust he was hurled across the wasteland and fell in a filthy heap on the ground. Miraculously not a single piece of brick had touched him and apart from being grey instead of black and having a dreadful headache, he was completely unharmed.

The tower was not unharmed. When the dust had cleared Bert could see the magnificent building was now nothing more than a sad pile of broken bricks. He remembered all the days he had sat on the top of the tower with his family and his mates looking out across the whole town. On clear summer days you could see right into the countryside, see the soft green hills rolling away into a distant blue haze and in the other direction the hills turned to valleys that slipped softly down to the sea. It was all so sad.

For three weeks men with lorries cleared the broken tower away. Bert sat on a nearby factory every day and watched them. He felt that until every single brick had gone he ought to watch over the last days of the three-hundred-foot chimney. He knew that it was what he had to do.

When the last lorry left Bert flew up into the sky above the tower's ghost and when he reached the place where the top had been he looked down at the ground. And there below him was the sandwich and still holding on to it was the rat. Only now the sandwich was no longer a white speck, it was as wide as a double bed and the rat was as long as a carpet and compared to them the two-metre hedgehog, true or not, seemed as thick as Eddie.

Bert drifted slowly down on the warm air taking in the wonderful sight of the flattest meal there had ever been in the whole history of any universe. For nearly an hour he floated round and round until at last he landed in the middle of the most perfect meal he had ever seen, a meal so thin that to anyone else it would have been invisible. He flew around its edge in both directions. He flew back up into the sky for one last look and then when the afternoon sun had warmed it all to perfection he came down to eat.

Venus the Caterpillar

Venus the caterpillar crawled out from under the tomato plant leaf in the greenhouse and looked up at the stars. Low in the evening sky was a thin silver crescent, too small to cast a shadow but as delicate as a piece of fine jewellery. Venus had never seen the moon before and she couldn't take her eyes off it.

'It's the most beautiful thing I've ever seen,' she said, but no one seemed very interested.

'Oh yes?' sneered Gilbert the cockroach. 'And what other beautiful things have you seen?'

'Leaves,' said Venus, 'and stalks and other things.'

'Like what?' said Gilbert.

'A flowerpot,' said Venus. 'I've seen a flowerpot.'

'You're pathetic,' said Gilbert and scuttled off to eat some compost.

The next night the moon had grown and the night after that it grew more. In fact, it kept growing for days and days until it was as big and round as the sun. And as it grew it began to cast a cool blue light over the world. When it was full, its beams poured down through the trees and sent long dark shadows across the lawn, bathing the whole world in peaceful silence. Everything looked frozen in its cool glow. Even the tomatoes above Venus's head shone blue like little moons themselves. She looked up through the leaves and knew that no matter what she did she had to go to the moon. She didn't know that one day she would have wings and be able to fly. Nor did she know that when she could fly she would then find out just how incredibly far away the moon was. She just knew she had to go there.

'If I went outside,' she said, 'and climbed to the top of the tallest tree, right to the very end of the highest leaf, do you think I could reach it?'

'Oh yeah,' scoffed Gilbert, 'if you waited like a million years for the tree to grow until it was thousand million miles tall.'

'Really? That's great,' said Venus. 'How long's a million years?'

'Give me strength,' cried Gilbert, banging his head against a sleeping slug and getting his feelers all sticky.

'Well, how long is a million years?' said Venus. 'Is it longer than tomorrow and today all put together?'

Gilbert muttered something under his breath about wishing he was carnivorous and vanished. Venus couldn't see what all the fuss was about. It all seemed quite simple. By the time she got out of the greenhouse, the tree would have already grown quite a lot and by the time she climbed to the end of the very highest leaf, it probably would be a million years old.

'I suppose,' she said to anyone who would listen, 'there's always the possibility that the tree will grow faster than I can climb it and I suppose it could take so long to get there that by the time I do, the tree could be taller than the moon and I'd have to come down a bit.'

Gilbert was swearing underneath the table but Venus couldn't make out what he was saying. It didn't matter anyway. She didn't know that cockroaches were nasty sarcastic creatures. She just thought Gilbert was being helpful.

Venus said goodbye to all her brothers and sisters and set off straight away. She crawled down the tomato plant stalk, down the outside of the flowerpot and wriggled to the edge of the table. She stopped and looked back at her home, wondering if she'd ever see it or her family again. As she turned to go on, she glanced up at the beautiful moon and almost fainted.

It was shrinking. All down one side it had vanished. Venus couldn't believe it. Her great big beautiful moon was dying and it was dying so fast that it would be gone before she could get there.

'If only I could reach it in time,' she said, 'I might be able to make it well again.'

'You are the most stupid caterpillar I've ever met,' said Gilbert. 'No, wait a minute. That's not true. Every caterpillar I've ever met, and I've met hundreds, has been just as stupid as you are.'

'But the moon is dying,' said Venus.

'No it isn't,' said Gilbert. 'It does that every month. It gets bigger and then it gets smaller and then it gets bigger again.'

'Are you sure?' said Venus.

'Are caterpillars horrid little creatures that look like the outsides of their bodies are missing? Of course I'm sure,' said Gilbert.

'So if I climb the tree it will come back again and I'll be able to go there?' said Venus.

'Yeah, yeah, sure,' said Gilbert and scuttled off again.

'Why do I keep doing this?' he said as he hurried across the greenhouse floor. 'Why do I keep having all these conversations with these idiots? Why don't I stay at home and do something I'd enjoy more like hitting my head against the wall?'

Venus slipped over the edge and began to crawl towards the floor, but when she reached the underneath of the table a strange feeling began to come over her. It was a feeling that she had never felt before, a sort of weird feeling that something incredible was going to happen.

Isn't it lovely under here? she thought, even though she couldn't see her beloved moon. *I think I'd like to have a little sleep right where I am.*

Part of her thought she should go on. After all, it was quite a long way to the moon so she shouldn't waste any time. But a stronger feeling seemed to be overtaking her and that told her it was time for bed. The more she tried to sort out her thoughts, the more tired she became until she just had to go to sleep. She spun a tiny silk thread, fixed it to the underneath of the table and soon fell fast asleep. And as she slept, strange and incredible things happened to her.

Venus the moth yawned and stretched. Inside her head she was still Venus the caterpillar but on the outside she was now Venus the moth. Of course, she didn't know this yet. She still thought she was a caterpillar and than she had just nodded of to sleep for a bit. It had been dark when she had gone to sleep and it was still dark, so she thought it was the same day. In fact, a whole winter had passed. She had gone to sleep in the autumn and now it was early spring.

Better get on, I suppose, she thought to herself and stretched to her full length. *Got to get to the moon.*

Suddenly there was a loud splitting noise and Venus felt a blast of cool air. She felt blood moving through places she didn't remember having. There were hairs all over her body where she had been smooth and shiny.

'I'm sure they weren't there when I went to sleep,'

she said, peering back at a pair of pale wings. 'I'd have noticed them.'

She waved the new wings and found she was hovering in mid air.

Oh wow, she thought. *This is incredible.*

And she realised that she wouldn't have to climb all the way up the tree to reach the moon. She could just fly there. It was brilliant.

'I won't have to wait a million years any more,' she said. 'I'll just be able to fly there in half an hour.'

She looked up into the sky and there was the beautiful moon. Only it looked different from before. When she had been a caterpillar, it had seemed enormous and had looked as if it was an extremely long way away. Now she was a moth it looked quite small and very close.

Funny that, she thought and flew up to the top of the greenhouse roof for a better look. And it was very close and instead of being cool and blue it was now warm and pale gold and it had a name and its name was 40 Watts.

'It's even more beautiful close up,' said Venus.

Every night she flew to the moon. Every night she flew round and round it and the amazing thing was that it never got smaller ever again. Venus knew then that Gilbert the cockroach had been wrong. All that stuff about the moon getting bigger and smaller had just been rubbish. The moon had been dying and she knew that by flying up to it she had made it well again. After all, if that wasn't the case then why would she have woken up with a pair of wings?

Moonlight

The sky has no clouds on this dark night
And people sleep deep in their beds.
Children are dreaming
And the dogs at their feet
Run through old days in their heads.

The sky has no clouds but millions of stars,
Other suns with worlds of their own.
Round each one a moon
Might look down through its trees.
So why do we feel so alone?

The sky has no clouds on this dark night
And moonlight runs over the town.
Its shadows are dark
Giving places to hide
As the owl flies across looking down.

The sky has no clouds but millions of stars,
And a dog looks up at the moon
And it howls at the light
Like its ancestors did
For the spine-chilling dawn coming soon.

Ethel's Dreamtime

The long hot summer began to slip away. At first it was barely noticeable, no more than a slight fading of the trees and a softness in the grass as if nature was getting tired and wanted a rest. Plants that had stood tall and proud began to hang their heads and give up their seeds to the wind. Ethel the chicken felt tired too. Autumn was creeping into her bones and like the plants, she felt weary. Like them she had grown old and slow. She had seen it all before many times and now she just wanted to sleep.

'You're the oldest animal in the garden,' said Arthur the rabbit. He had lived for twelve years and all his life Ethel had been there. Even back in his earliest memory she had been old.

'In fact,' he said, 'you are probably the oldest chicken in the world.'

Ethel didn't really understand what Arthur was talking about. She was a chicken and being old didn't mean anything to her. Yesterday was just like last week only not so fuzzy round the edges. A few things remained in her memory. There was Eric the cockerel who had been so proud and strong and there was a picture in her mind from long ago of an old lady stroking her head. And she could remember a time when the grass had grown tall and the garden had become a jungle. They had been exciting days. All the other animals had thrived in those years and many new creatures had come to live in the garden, but Ethel had felt lonely. The house had been empty apart from rats and spiders. The windows had been dark every night and the doors had stayed locked and closed.

'It all feels so lonely without anyone living here,' she had said.

'It's peaceful,' said the other animals, 'and safe.'

'I miss them,' said the old chicken.

'You just miss the food,' said the others.

'No,' Ethel had said. 'It's not the food. It's the talking. I miss the warm voices and the feeling of belonging to someone.'

'Animals shouldn't belong to anyone,' said the others. 'We're wild animals, we should be free.'

'I don't want to be wild or free,' Ethel had said. 'I want to belong to someone.'

Nothing the other animals said had made any difference. She'd heard them tell her about all the terrible things that people did to animals but she had never seen any of it so it didn't really mean anything. The only humans she had ever known had been kind and she had missed them.

'It's because I'm domesticated,' she used to say sadly, without really knowing what it meant.

Then everything had changed. A family had come to live in the house and the loneliness had ended. The man had given her a smart new box to live in and the children had come to see her every day. Later on they gave her eggs to hatch and she had children again, four beautiful hens called Doris and a magnificent cockerel called DorisBoris. They had their grown-up feathers now and scratched and fussed around the garden all day. They had seen their own seasons and didn't need her any more.

The children in the house were growing up too. Every day they brought her food and every day they tickled her behind the head. She sat in the thick warm straw in the dark end of the chicken hut and waited for them to come. Sometimes when the day was warm and the air buzzed with the hum of summer, one of the children would carry her up to the house and she would potter about in the flower beds while they sat on the steps reading books. But now winter was coming and the children stayed indoors.

'I feel so tired,' said the old chicken. 'Even when I wake up, I feel tired.'

'It's getting old does that,' said Arthur the rabbit. 'I feel the same. You need to sleep more.'

'That's all I ever do anyway,' said Ethel. 'Sleep.'

But it wasn't true. She sat still a lot but she found herself sleeping less and less. As the sun went down her children came back into the hut to roost. One by one they hopped up onto the perch and huddled together clucking and muttering to themselves until they fell asleep. It was a gentle friendly noise and the air smelt warm and comfortable but in her box at the other end of the hut Ethel sat staring through the window at the night sky. During the night the mice and rats would shuffle through the straw on the floor looking for scraps of food. Sometimes they would stop and talk to Ethel but most nights they were too busy and ignored her. On cloudless nights an owl would fly past, its shape outlined against the moon. Ethel saw the face on the moon and she watched the stars move silently over the world as they had done for millions and millions of years. And if there were no stars she stared into the darkness until morning.

It had become the same every night. Sleep had left her and it had left her tired. Sometimes in the warm afternoon sunshine she would nod off for a while but the slightest thing would wake her and that would be the end of it. But it was winter now and there was no sunshine warm enough for dreams.

'I just don't seem to be able to get warm any more,' she said.

'That's old age too,' said Arthur. 'Your heart gets slow. Your blood gets thin and stands still.'

'I don't think I want any of that,' said Ethel.

'Any of what?' asked Arthur.

'Old age.'

'Well, it isn't something you can decide about,' said Arthur. 'It just happens.'

'What, even if you don't want it to,' said Ethel.

'Yes, of course,' said Arthur.

'Who told you that?' said Ethel.

'My father,' said Arthur.

'Is that what happened to him?' said Ethel. 'Did he get old age?'

'Yes.'

'And is it like that for everyone?'

'I think so,' said Arthur.

'You mean, I'm going to be tired and cold forever?' said Ethel.

'I don't know,' said Arthur irritably. He was tired too and he didn't feel like talking about it.

Ethel sat silently in the door to the hut. She wanted to ask Arthur about his father. If he still had old age and if he found it difficult to sleep but Arthur limped off into the bushes. Perhaps she should go and talk to Arthur's father. Perhaps he could tell her what was going to happen.

She sat there staring into space and her thoughts all faded away. Daydreaming, that's what her mother had called it.

'Stop daydreaming,' she'd said, when Ethel had been young and feeling all lazy in the sunshine.

'Why?' Ethel had asked. Her mother had never had a really good answer for that, but it had left Ethel with a feeling that sitting around doing nothing was wrong and all her life she had felt a bit guilty about doing it. Now she didn't care. Now, as she let her thoughts drift away, they really did drift away and her head became completely empty and her eyes grew lazy until everything was a blur. The sweet emptiness made up for the lack of sleep. She felt as if she could sit there forever.

'Come on, out of the way,' shouted a voice in her ear. 'Move over, some of us have got work to do.'

It was one of her daughters, pushing past her. Ethel fell over and the younger hen ran into the hut and laid an egg.

'There's no need to rush,' said Ethel, struggling to her feet and fluffing out her feathers. 'There's more to life than laying eggs.'

'No there isn't,' said her daughter.

'Of course there is,' said Ethel. 'What about sunsets and the smell of the rain on the grass? What about daydreaming?'

'Daydreaming, daydreaming?' said her daughter. 'What a waste of time.'

'What about flowers and talking to your friends? What about bacon rind?' said Ethel.

'You're going soft in the head,' said the young hen. 'You're just saying that because you can't lay eggs any more.'

'No I'm not,' said Ethel, but she wasn't really sure.

'You're just saying that because you're old and useless,' said the young hen and crashed off into the bushes.

Ethel stood staring at the floor. Maybe her daughter was right, maybe that was what life was all about, just laying eggs. The old hen climbed down from the shed and shuffled through the long grass to the pond. That was where she always went when she was feeling low.

She ignored the rabbits under the tall trees. Other animals called out good mornings as she went by but she didn't notice any of them. She dragged her feet in the earth, looked out across the canal and sighed deeply. When she reached the pond she walked in up to her knees and stood ankle deep in the mud. She stood there for hours staring at her her own reflection in the water.

'Do you think I'm old and useless?' she said to the reflection, but it said nothing.

The little creatures wriggled between her toes, as they always did, and, as always when she was miserable, she didn't notice them. Old thoughts came into her head and she remembered the feeling she had had many years ago. It was loneliness.

It was different this time. The loneliness she had felt before had been because there had been no one to love her. Now she had that. The children came every day. Wherever she was in the garden, they came and found her and carried her back to the hut and fed her. The loneliness she felt now was deep inside, a sadness for the years gone by, a dull pain for all the things she would never see again.

One of the toads came and stood beside her. He sat down in the water and looked up at Ethel.

'Beautiful, isn't it?' he said.

'What?' said Ethel.

'All this,' said the toad.

'All what?' said Ethel.

'This,' said the toad, 'The water, the mud, all this.'

'It's horrible,' said Ethel. 'I only come here when I'm depressed.'

'Ooh, someone got out of the nest on the wrong side this morning, didn't they?' said the toad.

'Don't be stupid, warty,' said Ethel. 'There's only one way to get out of my nest.'

'What do you know? You're just a useless old chicken,' said the toad and disappeared into the water.

Ethel felt worse than ever. She couldn't even be miserable in peace. She went and sat on the compost heap, but it was no better. As soon as she sank into the warm slimy cabbage leaves on the top, three slugs wriggled out and started telling jokes about chickens crossing roads. Ethel ate them but it didn't make her feel any better.

She walked round the edge of the lawn until she reached the back of the house. It was deserted. The French windows were open and there was music coming from inside the room but there was so sign of anyone. Even Rosie the dog was nowhere to be seen.

Ethel clambered up the steps and looked in the doorway. It had been years since she'd been inside the house. She had forgotten all about it and now standing there, it all came flooding back. She had been young then, sometimes even laying more than one egg a day, and the old lady had been living there then. The room had been darker then and had smelt as old as the lady. Now it was bright and clean. In her youth Ethel had been inside sometimes. The old lady had given her cake crumbs and then carried her out into the garden again.

The old chicken walked into the room and stood in the middle of the carpet. It was soft and gentle like the grass in dreams. There was a fire dancng and sparkling in the grate and the air was warm and peaceful. Ethel stood there and felt the sleep she had wanted for so long begin to creep over her. She looked round for somewhere to settle down but there were no nests anywhere.

She walked into the hall where the air was even warmer. Something from above seemed to reach out for her. It led her towards the stairs and one by one it led her slowly up the stairs. Her legs ached and each stair seemed taller than the last but finally she reached the top and stood in a long field of green carpet. Across the hall was a half-open door. It was dark and as inviting as a summer night and whatever it was that had called her upstairs seemed to be there inside the cupboard. She looked round the edge of the door and there in the twilight was a nest of delicate blue blankets. Ethel settled down into it and closed her eyes. Pictures of home drifted through her head, golden days when Eric the cockerel had stood beside her, summer days that had seemed to last forever. And there he stood, as tall and proud as her memory, silhouetted against the darkness.

'Eric, is that you?' she said.

Invisible arms reached out and stroked her feathers. She felt herself as light as clouds and Ethel the chicken knew at last that it was time to sleep.

The Twelve Thousand Franks

Under the lawn where the cut grass gave way to the jungle of weeds and bushes was an ants' nest. It had been there for as long as anyone could remember. It burrowed out in all directions, into the centre of the lawn itself and back into the dark tangle of fallen branches and dead leaves. Its tunnels were a never-ending bustle of activity. Twenty-four hours a day the ants were busy. Most other animals had time when they slept, but not the ants.

The mornings were worst. Living with thousands of other ants in such a small space was always noisy but at the start of the day the racket was deafening as the tunnels shook to the endless pounding of one hundred and forty-four thousand feet rushing off to work. Frank1942 didn't know the exact number but one hundred and forty-four thousand seemed like a fair guess. Of course Frank786 had lost one of his legs in a jam sandwich and there were several Sandras with two extra feet, but life was too short to be that fussy. If there were a thousand more or twenty-three less it would hardly make any difference. The noise was deafening and Frank1942 had a splitting headache.

'You're pathetic,' said anyone who would listen to him. 'Ants don't get headaches.'

'Well, I've got one,' said Frank1942.

'It's impossible,' said Sandra12996. 'You're just pretending to get off work.'

'Maybe I'm different,' said Frank1942. 'Maybe I've evolved into a new super ant.'

'What?' said Sandra12996. 'A wonderful new species that can get headaches?'

'Well, it could happen,' said Frank1942.

'A new race of ants, exactly the same as ordinary ants but with headaches,' laughed the others. 'That's brilliant.'

Frank1942 crept away down the tunnels to

another part of the nest where he had never been before. No one understood him. He was different from all the others. He knew it, but no one else did. He knew there was more to life than rushing off to work all day following everyone else. He knew there were things like poetry and thinking. Frank1942 had never told anyone about his poetry. They wouldn't understand, they'd just laugh at him. He tried to remember his best poems. They always cheered him up.

> *I wandered lonely as an ant*
> *That floats on high over tall ant hill*
> *When all at once I saw my mum*
> *Squashed inside an old phone bill.*

he sang, and

> *Jack and Jill went up the ant hill*
> *To fetch a big fat larva*
> *Jack fell down and broke his seventh knee*
> *And Jill creased up with laughter.*

and

Three blind ants, three blind ants
See how they run, See how they run
Smack into the wall.

He was still working on the last one.

'There must be more to life than this,' he said, but no one was listening.

Hundreds of ants rushed past him as he wriggled his way through the crowd in the opposite direction. His head hurt so much that he couldn't see properly. The faces of his thousands of brothers and sisters shoving past him became a blur until they all looked the same. He wanted to sit down and have a rest but there was nowhere to stop. The tunnels were filled with a wall to wall mass of busy insects.

At last, at five past nine, the rush began to ease off. Frank1942 staggered on until he could walk no further. The tunnels were almost deserted now, just a few stragglers running along to catch up with the rest.

'Hurry up, hurry up, we're late,' they called as they ran by.

Frank1942 found a crack in the tunnel wall and crept into it. He found himself in a cool dark cave full of roots and although his head was still hurting he soon fell asleep. In his dreams all his aches and pains faded away. The air fell silent and the tunnels were deserted. In his dreams he was the last ant on earth.

He had never been outside, up above the tunnels in the big world. He was only a second-class worker and wasn't allowed outside. But he had heard about it. He'd eavesdropped on the soldier ants talking about the sunshine and the trees and giant birds that could swallow you in one mouthful.

In his dreams he was out there right in the middle of a large red flower. He was standing ankle deep in a pool of sweet nectar. The sun shone down warm on his back and a gentle breeze drifted over the edge of the petals, tickling the hairs on his neck. It was paradise. No birds hovered in the air looking for an ant to eat. Birds, like everything else apart from Frank1942, no longer existed. For the first time in his life he was completely alone and it was wonderful. Well, he wasn't exactly alone. On another flower was a beautiful lady ant. Frank1942 slipped over the edge petal and crawled down the stalk towards the lady ant's flower. As he started to climb again, his dream exploded and he woke up to find the world crashing down around.

Sandra3687 looked out across the world. From the blade of grass she was hanging on to, a sea of green spread out in all directions right off into a distant haze. It was the first time she had ever been on the surface. Until that morning she had lived in the soft brown tunnels that spread out under the lawn. Each day she had rushed off to work with everyone else and hadn't even known that there was a world above. But then, with no warning, everything had changed. Suddenly the world had come crashing down and a few seconds later she had seen the sky.

She knew what had happened. Old ants had told of the day when The Gardener would come, when their world would come to a sudden and violent end. Sandra3687 had never believed it. She had thought it was just stories to make them work harder but now it had happened. The Gardener had come and punished them.

All around her in the relics of her home were the remains of her brothers and sisters. She alone had survived the disaster. She wondered about other parts of the nest, if it had been the same there, if she was now the only ant left alive in the world.

'Hello,' she shouted, but no one answered.

She climbed down from the grass and set off in no particular direction. She thought it best to get as far away from the broken nest as possible in case whatever had happened, happened again. There were some big red flowers in the distance and she set off through the grass towards them.

It was all new and frightening. The sky was filled with large dark shapes that covered the sun with giant shadows as they passed. Sandra3687 kept stopping and looking nervously over her shoulder. It wasn't being out in the world that was so scary, it was the fact that she was all alone. To make herself feel braver, she tried to think of all her brothers and sisters and pretend that they were just out of sight behind her. When she had felt afraid in the past she had always felt better when she recited her best poems. They always cheered her up.

Humpty Ant sat on the wall
Humpty Ant had a great fall
All the King's horses
And all the King's men
Trod on him.

she sang, and

Sweet Claire was a lovely young ant
Who was clever and quite elegant.
She said it's quite clear
I can see to next year
Because I am a Clairvoyant.

and,

Baa, baa, black ant
Have you any wool
Yes sir, yes sir,
No, hang on a minute.
No, of course I haven't
I'm an ant, stupid.

She was still working on that one.

'Hello, is there anyone there?' she called but there was no reply.

Frank1942 knew what had happened. The Gardener had come to punish them all for not working hard enough. Frank1942 shook the dust off his back and looked around. It was incredible, it was just like his dream. He had landed in the middle of a large red flower and the dust he had been covered in wasn't the remains of his home at all. It was sweet golden pollen. Like the dream, the sun was shining and a gentle breeze was blowing through the leaves. He looked around but unlike the dream there was no beautiful lady ant on another flower. He was all alone.

Perhaps she's been held up, he thought. *If I wait, she'll probably be along in a minute.*

'Hello, is there anyone there?' he called but there was no reply. He lay down in the warm sunshine and was soon fast asleep.

'Hello, is there anyone there?' Sandra3687 shouted but there wasn't. She picked her way through the tall grass all afternoon until at last she reached the clump of red flowers. She climbed up onto one of the petals and looked round, but she was all alone. She called again but there was no reply.

Hidden in the middle of his flower and fast asleep, Frank1942 heard nothing. He slept so deeply that even the thunderstorm that came in the evening didn't wake him. By then Sandra3687 had gone. She had run up a wooden plank, across an old chicken's foot and out of the garden to the canal bank. There she had found another ants' nest, changed her name to Muriel47889 and settled down to live happily ever after.

And as for Frank1942, hidden in the middle of his flower and fast asleep, the next morning a child picked the flower he was sleeping on and put it in a vase on the kitchen window sill. For the rest of his life Frank1942 lived in the back of a drawer in a home of dishcloths and sponges that tickled his feet. For breakfast he ate cake crumbs with marmalade and for dinner he ate cake crumbs with strawberry jam. Every evening he looked out through the window at the wild garden. Across the lawn the ants had built a new nest but it was too far away for Frank1942 to see it. Besides, he had no time to worry about what was going on outside. He had his poetry to work on and was far too busy trying to find new words that rhymed with ant.

Full Circle

In gardens all over the town people raked up gold and brown leaves into great piles and the evening air was filled with the soft sweet smoke of autumn bonfires. Birds tired from a summer raising children huddled in the branches and waited for winter.

And as it had done since the beginning of time, winter followed autumn and the days grew short and cold. The sun stayed low in the sky, its light weak and tired and it gave out so little heat that the heavy frost lay undisturbed from dawn to dusk. Every twig, every blade of grass, was held in suspended animation and an intense cold crept into every corner.

As the winter sank deeper into the earth so the animals that lived in its heart dug down below it. Some animals had flown away to warmer lands while those that were left did the best they could to survive. Some curled up in their beds and slept. Others sat it out and waited for spring.

Soon winter passed and the air was crowded with anticipation. Sleepers awoke, plants began to move and in the late spring it began to rain, not the destroying rain of winter but a hesitant rain that carried the promise of summer. A delicate uncertain rain fell in tiny drops, so small that you could barely see them. They hovered in the air like wet smoke, drifting down from clouds that were so thin the sun shone through them lighting everything with a dreamlike sparkle. The new grass twinkled as if every blade was made of glass and anyone who walked on it would break it. The children sat in the house, their chins resting in their hands, and stared out at the garden.

By the open French windows the children's grandfather, back from a life at sea, sat on a kitchen chair and smoked his pipe. The day was so peaceful that even the bees buzzed silently. Everyone felt themselves being lulled to sleep.

Through the open window came the wonderful smell of soft new rain on warm grass. It was that lush smell that first comes to you in your childhood and sits quietly in the back of your brain until you die. And for the rest of your life, every time it returns, it brings with it the same magic drawn up from the roots of the earth. It is the same smell that our most ancient ancestors, long before they walked on two legs and were human, caught in the mosses and ferns of the primeval swamps. It goes back far longer than that and tells you so by the shiver it sends down your spine. Its caressing softness filtered into the children's senses marking them forever, labelling them as two more specks in the palm of nature's hand.

Sunshine replaced the rain and the swallows came back from Africa. In great sweeping waves they flew across Spain and north over France. They swept across the sea and spread out along the south coast of England on the journey back to their old homes. As they moved northwards they split up into smaller and smaller groups. Last year's children followed their parents back to the nests where they had been born. Under bridges, in dark caves, in the roofs of barns and houses, wherever they had grown up, they made their new homes. They swooped low over water shaking off the last of the desert dust they had carried all the way from Africa.

Many years before, the old grandfather's sister had lived in the house with her old dog. When the dog had died she had moved away to live by the sea and for many years the house had stood sad and empty. Like the hibernating animals waiting for summer, so the house had waited for life to return to its rooms. Only Ethel, the old chicken, had been left behind. Only she had still been there when the old lady's nephew had brought his family to live in the house. Now Ethel was gone too but life never sleeps and Ethel's children still scratched and fussed about the garden. The old dog was buried beneath his favourite tree and on hot summer days, that was where Rosie took shelter from the midday sun.

The years passed, the grandfather went to live by the sea and the children grew up and moved away. Rosie's beard turned from brown to grey and Ethel's children had children of their own.

And through it all, the old house and its wild and wonderful garden grew older and older and as each year passed and each new coat of paint was added, generation after generation of children and animals made the house called fourteen their home.

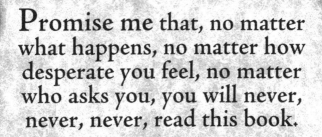